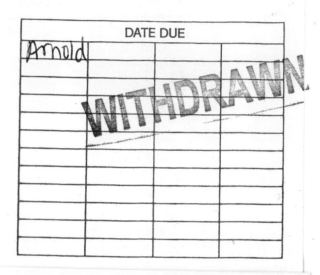

The Cinderella Game

The Cinderella Game

Jane Shore

AVALON BOOKS
THOMAS BOUREGY AND COMPANY, INC.
401 LAFAYETTE STREET
NEW YORK, NEW YORK 10003

J H O

PRINTED IN THE UNITED STATES OF AMERICA
BY HADDON CRAFTSMEN, SCRANTON, PENNSYLVANIA

The Cinderella Game

Chapter One

*S*ANDY was arranging a new display, the late-winter fabrics, when she happened to glance up and meet the eyes of a scruffy-looking young man through the window. They were nice eyes, she thought, pleasantly crinkled at the corners and a surprising shade of deep blue. He smiled. Sandy smiled back, then got on with the job at hand and forgot all about him.

This business of arranging the displays was tricky. She was not allowed to cut into the yardage, so it was a matter of manipulating the bolts in a way that drew attention to the individual fabrics and suggested their purpose. She had spread white batting over the floor and sprinkled it with glitter. Now she was arranging the pastel plaids over a dark framework that she hoped would suggest a bare tree. She scooped up a handful of fabric, secured it with a pin, and sat back on her heels. It was hardly her finest effort, but it would do.

There was a trick to backing out from the win-

1

dow. You had to inch along on your knees, being careful not to disturb the finished display. It required concentration. Sandy was always relieved when she had both feet safely on the floor again.

As she straightened up, she saw that a customer was already waiting for her. It was the blue-eyed man and he looked ludicrously out of place among the piles of elegant fabrics. This could hardly be a man who cared for clothes. His jeans were faded and clumsily patched. He carried a grimy knapsack slung over his left shoulder, and he wore a baggy sweater instead of a winter coat. Yet he was examining a table of dress fabrics with passionate, if somewhat bewildered, interest. Sandy smoothed down her smock, tucked an errant strand of hair behind her ear, and went around to the other side of the table.

"Can I help you?" she asked.

He scratched his face ruefully. "I'm not sure. I know so little about these sorts of clothes. I need a dress, you see."

"A dress for a woman?" The man was young, but he didn't look married. Sandy couldn't have explained exactly what constitutes a properly married look, but this man presented such a grubby, neglected appearance. None of the buttons on his shirt matched; they had not even been sewn on with the same color thread. If he had a wife or a mother, Sandy decided, she could hardly be the kind of woman for whom one would buy dress fabric, unless perhaps he wanted to reform her. That didn't sound like a sensible project, but her job was to sell fabric.

"How old is the lady?" she asked politely.

"Very young," he said, frowning thoughtfully. "Not much over eighteen. She might be as young as seventeen, but I don't think she should be younger than that."

Sandy waited patiently. As a description of the woman in his life, this was too vague to be helpful. "How tall is she? And what about her coloring?"

"Medium height." He vaguely indicated the air in front of his chin. "We haven't decided on the coloring yet. Blond and black are too obvious. How do you feel about light-brown hair, something like yours?"

"My hair has the advantage of being attached to my scalp." Sandy felt her patience wearing thin. "Why don't you wait until the lady decides what color hair she wants, and then you can bring her here to pick out the fabric for her dress."

"I can't leave that decision up to someone else," he protested. "She'll probably have to wear a wig anyway. Now, assuming we can find a nice golden-brown wig, something like your hair, what do you think would be a good color for the dress?"

"Is it for a special occasion?" Sandy was getting interested in this unlikely customer. He was so very odd.

"A ball gown, of course," he said, as though this were the most common kind of garment. "Bell-shaped, with hoops or petticoats, and perhaps a train. Cut very low at the neck and pinched in at the waist. You know the sort of thing."

"A formal," Sandy suggested. "A prom dress maybe?"

He shook his head impatiently. "Oh, no, nothing like that. It has to be resplendent, not just pretty. Nothing sugary, no pastels. They wash out under the lights. And I don't want white. That's become a cliché. Do you think we could get away with a good bright tomato red?"

"I can show you several bolts of red silk," Sandy offered eagerly, seeing a chance for a magnificent sale. "I'm sure the lady would like pure silk. It has so little weight, drapes beautifully, takes dye like no other fiber, and you can't beat the feel of it. Pure silk is the ultimate in luxury."

"Pure silk?" He looked horrified. "That would never do. It wouldn't stand up to the wear and tear. What we need is something sturdy. It mustn't wrinkle or go limp on us, and it must be washable."

"We carry some washable silks," Sandy suggested doubtfully. "Many of our customers prefer to hand wash silk garments, rather than send them to a dry cleaner."

"Hand washing's no good," the young man said briskly. "We have to be able to toss everything into the washing machine. One of those synthetics would probably be best. They make brocades out of nylon, don't they?"

"And from Dacron too," Sandy admitted, sighing at the thought of such a utilitarian ball gown. "If you will come to the back of the store, I'll show you what we have in that line."

In the middle of the shop, Mrs. Roberts sat at the cash register, delicately riffling through a pile of invoices as another woman might have fingered a bouquet of roses. The manager's pale blue hair was arranged in a pompadour so stiffly sprayed that it looked like a cage of spun aluminum. A pencil was stuck through the apex of this edifice. Mrs. Roberts's purple mouth was tightly pursed, and her eyes glittered like jet beads.

"Don't waste your time, Miss Childs," she hissed as they passed her. "Sell, sell, sell."

The young man caught Sandy's eye and grinned. "Maybe I'd better let you sell me something," he suggested. "Your boss doesn't hold with socializing on the job."

Sandy smiled back. "Neither do I, for that matter. I intend to sell you six or seven yards of red brocade, not to mention the findings, thread, hooks, buttons, featherboning, braid, lining fabric, zippers—and, of course, a pattern."

"A pattern?" he said doubtfully. "Am I going to need that?"

She regarded him with exasperated pity. "You'll need either a pattern or a designer."

Instead of being cast down, he gave her the happiest of smiles and slapped his right palm against his forehead. "A designer, of course. Why didn't I think of that right away? Thank you, oh, thank you. You are an angel, Miss Childs. That is your name, isn't it? At least, I think that's what the dragon lady called you."

"Sandra Childs," she said, holding out her hand. "I'm glad I was able to help, although I'm darned if I know what I did. Are you sure you don't want to bring in the lady to look at the patterns?"

"No need," he said cheerfully. "As you pointed out, a good designer will take care of everything."

Sandy heaved a sigh of regret. "I was hoping you'd buy a pattern from us, and the fabric."

"I will," he assured her, grinning. "I promise to buy the fabric from you and from no one else. And it will be twice as much as you said, because we will need two ball gowns."

"Two exactly the same?"

"Of course. We can't have the poor girl shivering in her petticoats while her dress is swishing around in the washing machine. And there will probably be mending to be done. Things do tear." He looked down at his left knee, which sported several layers of patches. "Yes, I think we'd better have two."

"Miss Childs! Miss Childs, to the front." The manager's voice cut through the air like a whip. "You have a customer, Miss Childs, if you please."

Sandy gave the young man a quick smile before turning to the stout woman who had just come into the store, dragging a chubby little girl behind her. The child looked utterly miserable.

"I don't want homemade clothes," she wailed. "Nobody else wears dresses. Why can't I wear jeans like everyone else?"

"Because dresses are kinder to your figure." The heavyset woman sounded discouraged. Sandy's heart went out to her. She looked so very tired. Shopping with children could be hard work.

"I'm not fat," the little girl asserted. "Just because you are, you think everybody else is too. I don't need dresses. I need jeans."

"Of course you're not fat, darling." The mother sounded close to tears. "You look very nice, but I do think—"

Edging past the young man, Sandy squared her shoulders and sailed into the middle of the fray.

"We just got some new patterns in," she announced. "I'm sure we can find something both of you will like."

"I want jeans," the little girl grumbled.

The mother was getting increasingly flustered. "But you look so much prettier in dresses."

"Miss Childs, show the ladies our new line of stretch denims," Mrs. Roberts shrilled.

The young man had meanwhile worked his way to the door. Sandy could feel his eyes on her, and she had to put up her hand to stifle a giggle.

Mrs. Roberts, however, had obviously had enough of this ragged person who looked so out of place in her little shop. She approached him with the air of a good housekeeper intent on removing some offending substance. "Is there something we can do for you?"

He turned to her with overblown courtesy, which seemed particularly ridiculous coming from this shabby scarecrow of a man.

"I am in need of fourteen, maybe as much as twenty yards of red brocade," he announced. "I will also need buttons, hooks, zippers, featherboning and a great deal of thread. Miss Childs understands exactly what I require. Since she is busy just now, I will return when she is not engaged."

He swept the astonished manager a formal bow and stalked out of the shop.

Mrs. Roberts's Sew Nice Boutique was on the top level of the Randolph Shopping Mall, tucked between Gladstone Jewelry and His-N-Hers Sportswear. The mall was enormous and boasted several bigger fabric shops. What distinguished Sew Nice—and kept its customers coming back—was partly the unusual fabrics and trims it stocked but mostly the delightful Miss Childs. It was a rare thing these days, the older customers told each other, to find a young woman who seemed to like her job. Miss Childs was patient, energetic, well-informed, and helpful. Unlike the dreaded Mrs. Roberts, Miss Childs seemed to like people. Moreover, she understood clothes. You came into the shop frazzled and uncertain, and you left with the happy feeling that your purchase was exactly what you had been looking for. If something was going to shrink or fade, Miss Childs could be trusted to warn you. If the color was wrong, she would tell you so, in the gentlest, kindest way possible. And she was so pretty, with her big brown eyes, warm apricot-colored skin, and that soft mop of dark-gold hair. The jade-green smock that looked so preposterous stretched over Mrs. Roberts's pouter pigeon figure billowed delightfully from Miss Childs's slim shoulders and floated behind her as she ran back and forth, trying to satisfy everyone.

The shop never closed its doors until the last customer had made a leisurely selection. The sign on the door said nine-thirty to six, but it was usually half an hour later before Sandy locked the door behind her.

This meant that her friend Meg, who worked for a realtor on the lower level, had to wait to drive her home. Meg and Sandy shared a small apartment and a closetful of clothes. Meg owned the car.

"I don't know why you put up with it," Meg grumbled. "Let's get out of here before they lock up the place for the night. Does the old battle-ax pay you overtime, at least?"

"No, she doesn't," Sandy admitted, then grinned at a sudden memory. "A man referred to her as the dragon lady today."

"A man?" Meg brightened. "Do you have men coming in to buy fabric?"

"This one didn't buy anything."

"Probably lost his way," Meg decided. "Hurry up. Al's picking me up at eight. Do you have any plans for tonight?"

"Well, yes."

Meg groaned. "Not Peter Brooks again."

Sandy nodded.

"Why in heaven's name do you waste your time on that jerk? He's a loser."

"For one thing, because he went to school with my brother, and because he really is a nice, decent guy."

"And because nobody else asks you out," Meg said brutally.

"And that," Sandy agreed calmly, "is another good reason."

Meg sang along with the car radio as she drove, and Sandy closed her eyes and thought about her date for the evening. Pete was dull. There was no denying it. He had only three interests in life. One was his job as bookkeeper for Brae-Mill, manufacturers of ladies' sportswear.

Pete had a solid future with them, and his job absorbed him for eight hours a day, five days a week. His other passion was baseball, which kept him happily occupied throughout the season. In winter, however, when the football players took over the stadium, he had nothing to distract him from his third-ranking interest, Sandra Childs.

"What does he talk about?" Meg wanted to know. "Every time I've seen him, he's asked me about my job, and then he's told me about his. No, wait a minute, I'm not being fair. There was one day last summer when he actually mentioned the weather. A game had been rained out, and he was very upset."

"He likes baseball," Sandy agreed mildly.

"You don't mind going to see the Indians every single week? Wouldn't you like to go to a disco some night, or a movie, or even a wrestling match? How about restaurants, concerts, plays?" Meg was getting excited. "There are other things in life besides baseball, you know."

"I know."

"So, get out there and find them. You're going to be a shriveled old woman someday, and all you will be able to tell your great-grandchildren is 'Great-grandpa used to take me to the game.' "

"Pete happens to like baseball," Sandy said with a smile. "And I have no intention of marrying him."

"Don't you be too sure," Meg warned her

darkly. "You've been dating him for over a year. How often does he propose?"

"Once a month on the average."

"One of these days, my friend, you'll forget to shake your head, and before you know it you'll be raising a team of Little Leaguers. I can just see it."

The apartment Meg and Sandy shared was cheap—and with good reason. It had started life as the kitchen and servants' quarters of a Victorian mansion, which was now converted into apartments. At first glance their apartment was little better than a basement, and on closer examination it was rather worse. Gravy-colored paint encrusted the woodwork, mildew stained the walls, and the windowsills were level with the pavement.

Sandy didn't mind. "We get a nice view of people's legs and feet."

"I'd rather have a penthouse and look down on the tops of their heads." Meg hated the apartment. "The trouble with you, Sandra Childs, is that you have no aspirations. Look at the way you stick with that job! It doesn't pay. There's no future in it, and you never meet any interesting people. Do you think I would have met Al if I'd been working in a fabric shop?"

"Probably not," Sandy agreed, "but you know how I feel about fabric. As soon as I've saved up enough to take some courses at the Art Institute—or if I could go to Paris. . . . Do you realize that they take on women as apprentices over there?" Her eyes were dreamy. "Places like Dior and Balmain. Imagine!"

Meg snorted disdainfully. "And when all's said and done, what would you be—a dressmaker."

"Oh, no," Sandy said softly. "A designer."

"Nobody hires designers these days."

"Some people must hire them. Look, Meg, you can go out and buy a dress because somebody cut up fabric and sewed the pieces together. And before that, someone wove the cloth and made the pattern, and before that"—she took a deep, ecstatic breath—"somebody created the design."

"Most manufacturers buy their designs from Europe and have them made up in Hong Kong. Wake up, Sandy. You don't really want to be a dressmaker and spend your life putting up hems for women who are too stingy to go out and buy a new dress now and again. What you want is a fun job where you can make a bit of money and meet people."

"I do meet people."

"Oh, yeah? And how many of the people you meet are good-looking guys? When is the last time a hunk walked into that shop of yours and turned out to be in need of a designer?"

"As a matter of fact," Sandy said with a big grin, "that is precisely what happened today."

Chapter Two

*P*ETE Brooks announced his arrival with his special signal, three quick raps in succession, then two separate knocks. Like all Pete's little ways, it had been amusing at first but had become irritating. He was a stocky young man who took great pains with his appearance. There had been a time when Sandy had admired the way his socks, shirts, and ties harmonized with his wrinkle-free suits. By now his carefully coordinated outfits had become as predictable as his conversation.

"You're looking very pretty tonight," he said, as he always did.

"Thank you, Pete," Sandy said, as she always did. "Do come in. Would you like a drink?"

"I've brought some wine coolers," he announced proudly, as if this were a new departure. "It's not like real drinking, is it? I wouldn't want to get you into bad habits."

"I'll put them in the refrigerator. Shall we have dinner here, or would you like to go out?"

15

Pete allowed himself a portentous pause before informing Sandy that he loved her cooking. She was just a wonderful little cook, he told her.

"I'm warming up last night's spaghetti," Sandy offered without enthusiasm. "And there's some lettuce and a tomato or two."

Pete looked perturbed. "You didn't put garlic into the spaghetti sauce, did you? You know I can't eat garlic."

"It came out of a can, so I imagine it has garlic in it," Sandy said heartlessly. "I didn't make it from scratch. I didn't have time."

"I wish you'd give up your job." Pete gazed wistfully into her eyes. "You could move out of this rattrap and have a nice place of your own, time to cook decent meals, to putter about, to sew. . . . I know you like to sew."

"Oh, Pete," Sandy protested sadly. "Don't."

"But I want to take care of you," he persisted doggedly. "I can afford to support you in comfort. I'm due for another raise, and they have two-bedroom apartments in my building. I could have them reserve one for us, then we'd be all set."

"For the first of the Little Leaguers." Sandy made a choked sound in her throat, something between a sigh and a hiccup. "Meg did warn me."

"I don't understand why you won't—"

"Hush," Sandy said, laying a warning finger

across his lips. "You're rushing things. Your next proposal isn't due until next Friday."

Pete looked depressed, sniffed the garlic-laden fumes emanating from the kitchenette, and became even more lugubrious. "We'll have to send out for dinner," he decided sadly. "Shall I order chicken or pizza?"

"How about sushi?"

"Raw fish?" Pete was honestly horrified. "Do you have any idea how risky that is? Of course you're joking. I know you wouldn't really eat such stuff."

"I'd like a chance to try it someday," Sandy said wistfully.

Pete realized that he was up against female temperament, something he had heard about but never before encountered in his sane, sensible Sandy.

"Maybe you'd like to go out after all," he offered bravely. "There's a new Italian restaurant at Eastgate, where the rib place used to be. The guys at work were talking about it. They said it was quite nice."

Sandy was so overwhelmed that she gave him a hug. "Oh, Pete," she said, "you're a perfect knight in shining armor. I didn't really want to eat leftover spaghetti, with or without garlic."

The restaurant was crowded and had a hot, stale smell.

"Garlic," Pete whispered unhappily, as they

waited for the hostess. "The whole place reeks of garlic."

"A table for two?" the hostess fluted. "I'm afraid we can't seat you right away, since you don't have a reservation. Of course, if you'd care to wait?"

"We'll wait." Pete was glum but grimly determined to get his dinner.

"Why don't you take a seat in the bar," the hostess suggested. "I'll call you as soon as your table is free."

"But we don't want—" Peter started, but the hostess had already turned on her stiletto heel and floated away.

"Rude and inconsiderate," Pete muttered to himself, but he followed Sandy into the bar and sat down in the booth facing her. His face was red and unhappy.

"I had no idea," he began. "I wouldn't have brought you here if I'd known. . . . I don't like to subject you to a thing like this."

"Oh, for heaven's sake." Sandy was looking around with interest. "It's just for a few minutes."

"But sitting in the bar—it's not as if we wanted to drink."

"I'll have a glass of white wine," Sandy announced.

"But you don't—"

"I've never been in a bar before," Sandy explained. "Now that I'm here, I intend to enjoy myself."

Pete was astonished. That was one of the things he adored about Sandy. She was always coming up with odd, sometimes downright peculiar ideas. "How can you enjoy sitting in a dark, stuffy bar, waiting around for other people to finish their dinner?"

"I can kick off my shoes under the table for starters." Sandy did so and smiled blissfully. "And now I can wiggle my toes."

Pete was in agony. "Don't. Please don't."

Sandy patted his hand. "It's all right. No one can see my bare toes, which is just as well. They must be swollen to just about twice their normal size, poor things. I never got to sit down today. I didn't even get to take my lunch hour. It was that busy. Ah, that feels wonderful. I wonder if I could slip an ice cube between my toes."

"Please!" Pete begged.

"Okay, no ice cubes. You're quite right. It's not a good idea. I would drip all over the floor. Will you have a glass of wine too?"

Pete agreed miserably that he would, but cheered up somewhat when the glasses were placed in front of them. "Rather refreshing, isn't it? That was a good idea, Sandy. Now we don't look so odd, sitting here."

"But we're supposed to look odd," Sandy protested. "That's the least we can do for the people watchers."

"The what?"

"The people who come in here just to watch other people, like that man at the bar, the one with the handlebar moustache. I'd say he's a professional people watcher. Look at that thoughtful stare, that air of having a purpose in life."

"I think his purpose is merely to get bombed. I don't think he is looking at people at all. I don't think he can see them."

After a few minutes, Sandy had to admit that Pete was correct. The nose above the handlebar moustache was generously veined, and the eyes just north of the swollen nose had the glazed look of advanced alcoholism.

"You have a rare talent for people watching," she complimented Pete. "I'm impressed. Would you say he drinks for fun or because of a secret sorrow?"

"I don't care why he drinks," Peter protested. "Please stop staring at him. He's beginning to notice."

Sandy gave a last quick glance at the drinking gentleman. "I think he drinks to forget," she decided. "Perhaps he has been at it so long that he has forgotten what got him started. How about the couple at the end of the bar? Do you think they are deeply in love?"

"Sandy!"

"Well, they're too old not to be married, but the way they hold hands suggests. . . . Please stop kicking me. I'm sore enough already."

Pete was rescued by the hostess, who informed them in dulcet tones that she now had a table for them. There was a short delay while Sandy forced her swollen feet back into her shoes, but they were finally settled at a wobbly table uncomfortably close to the kitchen door. A frazzled-looking waitress came to take their order.

"We'll have the spaghetti with meat sauce," Pete said quickly, "and the house salad with oil and vinegar."

Sandy studied the menu carefully. "Is there anything without garlic?" she asked.

"Please," Pete begged, "don't make a fuss."

The waitress, however, was not at all disturbed by the question. "The veal marsala," she suggested. "They put scallions on top as a garnish, but there's no garlic in that. And the broiled lamb."

Pete cast a desperate glance at the right-hand column of the menu and hurriedly opted for the veal.

"How could you?" he said reproachfully, as soon as the waitress was gone. "What's gotten into you tonight?"

Sandy leaned back and examined him thoughtfully. "I've been thinking."

"Oh?" Pete was still stewing silently about the way the evening's expense was threatening to go through the ceiling.

"I've been thinking about us."

"It's about time," he grumped. "Do you realize we could be sitting comfortably in our own home, eating a decent, home-cooked, affordable meal, instead of listening to the clatter of pots and paying out a fortune for some sort of indigestible mess?"

"The veal may turn out to be delicious," Sandy said calmly, "but I agree with the din. It's horrid. We will have to ask for another table."

"They don't have one." Pete was sulky.

Sandy stood up, winced at the protest from her swollen toes, and wobbled painfully across the room to where the hostess was standing, gracefully poised on one foot, examining her perfect nails with dreamy contentment.

"We would like another table," Sandy said.

"Well, really," the hostess said, astounded. "After all, you didn't have a reservation. . . ."

"Quite." Sandy could sound almost as nasty as Mrs. Roberts when she put her mind to it. Her voice dripped ice. "And we are unlikely to come back in the future, with or without a reservation, unless you can find a better table for us."

The hostess tried to maintain her cool dignity, but Sandy was in enough pain to make her stubborn. "Well?" she demanded.

The hostess wilted. "I'll see what I can do. There are a few tables that are not entirely filled. Let me ask the people at the corner table if they would mind sharing. It is really a table for eight."

"That would be quite acceptable," Sandy pronounced with chilly grandeur, but she was grinning by the time she got back to Pete. "Success comes to those who face the enemy without flinching. We're being moved to the table in the corner."

"But those people are complete strangers."

"Either they will become acquaintances," Sandy said philosophically, "or we will ignore each other. It is a big enough table."

The corner table was indeed big enough to accommodate a large party. The two women already in possession looked up briefly, nodded, and went on with their conversation.

"This is very uncomfortable," Pete muttered. "I wish you hadn't. There are personal matters I want to talk to you about. How can we discuss—"

"We can't," Sandy interrupted calmly. "But you'll be able to enjoy your veal without the clatter of pots in your ears, and I will do the talking."

"You are talking a great deal tonight," he said huffily. "I've never known you to behave like this. What's gotten into you?"

At this point, the waitress brought their salads, and Pete became pleasurably occupied with food. Sandy, who was put off by the sight of tired lettuce leaves floating in a slick of oily dressing, crumbled a roll and regarded him thoughtfully.

"We've been spending too much time together," she announced abruptly. "That's what

I wanted to talk to you about. We're together once or twice a week. We don't have time to date other people. You should be meeting a lot of women."

"But I don't want to meet other women," Pete protested through a mouthful of salad.

"You need to look around."

"No, I don't. I've found the woman I want to marry."

Sandy realized that he was right in one way. This was not the place for the serious talk that had to take place. Her eyes on the tablecloth, she sat back, arranging and rearranging the pieces of bread in pleasing patterns. Averting her attention from Pete, who was chewing with intense concentration, she could not help but listen to the women at the other end of the table.

"Why don't you try out for it?" the older woman was saying. She was plump and pretty, her sleek gray hair tied back with a brilliant silk scarf strangely at odds with her baggy, colorless turtleneck sweater. It was as if she had taken great pains with her head, and ignored everything from the shoulders down.

The younger woman was a different type altogether, so heavily made up that her face appeared to be lacquered. She wore a glitzy cocktail dress, much too formal for this setting. Her black hair was cut very short, and it was so stiff with mousse that it bristled out like a porcupine's quills.

"It's not really my bag," the younger woman said. "And as you say, there's no money in it."

"Think of it as an investment in your future," the older woman urged. She had a marvelous voice, deep and warm. "It's always good to have a variety of credits. You've never done any legit work, have you?"

Sandy was rather shocked. It did not seem right to listen in while a couple of crooks planned a crime. The next sentence reassured her.

"I did a walk-on once in a play," the black-haired woman said. "That didn't pay much either, and the play closed after three performances."

"I've done a few of those." The gray-haired woman laughed. "Last year I was in a turkey called *The Trouble with Emily.* The trouble with Emily was that the audience didn't care whether she lived or died. She died on the road—which of course is the reason for my being currently at rest. Nobody's auditioning for anything. My unemployment is good for another month or two, and Jason's such a dear. It would be a good opportunity for you to rack up a bit of experience."

"But it's not a professional production, and I don't like to get mixed up with amateurs."

"Semiprofessional, darling. Jason used to direct summer theater, did rather good work too. Of course he's no longer in the theater full-time, poor boy, but he has a knack. If he directs, it's unlikely to be unprofessional. The supporting parts are being filled with amateurs, but he promised to get pros for the leads. How about it?"

Sandy never got to find out what the black-haired woman's decision was going to be. The waitress arrived with their entrees, and the two women began to wrangle amiably about dividing up the check. By the time Pete had finished arranging the plates to his satisfaction and settled down to the business of demolishing his dinner, they were alone at the big corner table.

"Thank goodness they're gone," he said, putting down his fork. "Now we can talk. What was all that nonsense about wanting me to date other women? You know I'm not interested in anyone but you."

"I think you should be looking around."

"I see no reason for it." Pete managed to look both huffy and doggedly devoted. "I know what I want. Playing around's all right for boys, but I'm a grown-up man and ready to settle down. I can afford it, and I've found the woman I want. I simply don't understand why you suddenly suggest I start dating other women. As far as I am concerned, we have all that settled."

"It's not settled," Sandy insisted, "not for me. I'm sorry, Pete, but I don't feel settled."

"You're a lot younger than I am," Pete admitted tolerantly. "It won't make a whole lot of difference later on. In fact, it'll be rather nice. When I'm fifty, you'll be a sprightly forty-two. But it means you need more time to make up your mind."

"I have made up my mind, and I don't want to marry you."

Pete was so upset that he almost dropped his fork. As it was, it remained hanging from his fingertips, poised halfway between his mouth and the plate. "You're kidding."

Sandy took a deep breath. "I shouldn't have let this thing go as far as it did. Look, we only started dating because of my brother. I suppose Bill suggested you look me up. Kid sister in town, all alone, needs someone to keep an eye on her. Right?"

"Well, yes, but. . . ."

"And I was grateful. You can get pretty scared when you're away from home the first time in your life, living at the Y, looking for a job, and watching your savings account shrivel."

"I gave you a call to oblige Bill, that's true. I always liked him, frat brother and all that, but then I took one look at you and that was that." He blinked, and his chin puckered up. "I haven't looked at another woman since. There wouldn't have been any point in it."

"Oh, Pete." Sandy felt helpless. "You're so nice. You deserve a wonderful woman."

"I've found her. You're wonderful."

"You need a wonderful woman who will think you're wonderful too."

"I know you like me," Pete insisted obstinately. "It's just a matter of time. You don't want to get tied down just yet. I understand. But in time you will want to settle down, and I'll be right here, waiting."

Sandy had a grotesque vision of Pete sitting with his fork poised in the air, year after year, waiting for her.

"Stop waiting," she said, forcing herself to sound colder than she felt. "There's no future in it. It's not that I'm too young to make a commitment. If the right man were to walk in this very moment, I'd be ready. I am not a child. But you're not the right man." She struggled to hold back the tears prickling behind her lids. "And, Pete, dear Pete, please believe me—I'm not the right woman for you, either."

Chapter Three

"**S**o you finally ditched him," was Meg's comment. "About time, if you ask me. Anyone else in the offing?"

Sandy shook her head.

"Al has a friend, a nice guy, lots of laughs. Shall I set up a foursome?"

"Not for the time being. I think I just want to spend some evenings at home by myself."

"You're going to turn into a couch potato."

"At least I'll be an independent spud. Thanks, Meg. I appreciate the offer, but I haven't had any breathing space for over a year. I want to get to know myself before launching out into a new social life."

Mrs. Roberts's hair was pink this week. The glazed-egg shape of the structure was permanent, but the color varied.

"I want you to work out a cruise theme for the window," she announced even before Sandy had hung up her coat. "We have a new line of chalky slubbed linens that I want to push. Take care of that customer, will you? And then you can talk to me about your suggestions."

Sandy sold the customer two-and-a-half yards of corduroy, then returned to Mrs. Roberts, who was still perched behind her cash register like a spider.

"Well," Mrs. Roberts demanded, looking up irritably, "have you come up with anything?"

"Cruise clothes suggest a boat. We could hang up three life buoys and drape the linens through them, then arrange them in folds, like waves, in front."

"Unoriginal," Mrs. Roberts snapped, "but I guess it'll have to do."

"Can we rent the life buoys?"

Mrs. Roberts looked ready to faint. "Rent them? Really, Miss Childs, you must think we have a Rockefeller operating budget. There's plenty of canvas, padding, and paint in the stockroom. You can certainly make something that looks like a life buoy if you put your mind to it. And while we are at it—that woman bought only two-and-a-half yards of fabric. Surely you could have persuaded her to take at least four yards."

"Two-and-a-half was all she needed."

"Nonsense. It's always better to buy a few yards extra, just to be safe. I sometimes wonder if you are in the right profession. Sell, sell, sell."

"Yes, Mrs. Roberts," Sandy agreed obediently. "I'll be in the back making life buoys. Call if you need me."

She had managed to create three creditable white rings, wound about with cord that could easily pass for rope at a distance, when Mrs. Roberts's voice floated through the door:

"Miss Childs, come here at once."

Sandy propped up her works of art to dry and went into the shop, wiping her hands as she went.

"This gentleman insists on talking to you." Mrs. Roberts sounded deeply offended. "It seems he has already explained to you exactly what it is that he is looking for."

The young man with the dark blue eyes looked every bit as disreputable today. Instead of torn jeans, he was wearing a pair of corduroys that had long since given up both nap and color. He was quite a tall man, but that sweater had surely been made for a giant. It hung about him like a tent, sleeves almost to his fingertips and the raveled edge halfway to his knees. An enormous woolen scarf was untidily wrapped around his neck and dangled almost to the floor behind him. He looked so utterly absurd that Sandy found herself smiling broadly.

"Ah, you remember me," he said, looking pleased.

"Two tomato-red ball gowns," Sandy said. "Nipped waists, low décolletage, the skirts draped over hoops."

"Right," he agreed. "Let's have a look at your machine-washable, abuse-proof, indestructible ball-gown materials. I'll need about twenty yards."

"Twenty yards," Mrs. Roberts exclaimed, her eyes misting over at that magic number. "Please take your time. Miss Childs will show you what we have in stock, and if you don't find what you want, we'll be happy to place a special order for you."

"I've suddenly become popular." The young man looked astonished.

"You said twenty yards," Sandy explained. "That makes you a serious customer. Now you may even sit down."

"No time for that," he said briskly. "I haven't even come to buy the fabric, just to pick up swatches."

"You are about to lose Mrs. Roberts's seal of approval. You'd better buy something."

"I'll pay for the swatches. Let's say a quarter of a yard of every red synthetic you have in stock."

Normally Sandy would have agreed without a qualm. Selling was, after all, what she was hired to do. But this man looked so shabby. He was obviously very short of cash. Sandy didn't want him to spend so much money.

"That would come to twenty-five dollars or more. Can you really afford to spend that much just on swatches?"

His eyebrows rose. "You are protecting me against foolish extravagance? How nice of you."

Sandy felt her face getting hot. "Well, I thought. . . ." Her voice trailed off.

"I've never met a girl who actually manages to blush," he said, delighted. "It must be a lost art, and it looks marvelous on you. It also sets off that enchanting smudge of white paint you wear on your nose. What have you been doing?"

"Building life buoys for the new display," Sandy explained, rubbing her nose with the back of her hand, which spread the smudge rather than getting rid of it. "Look, I'm trying to save you money. You could take just an eighth of a yard of all the fabrics you're interested in. Normally we give away swatches for free, but I'm afraid Mrs. Roberts might not agree in this case."

"I know," he sympathized. "I heard the lady—'sell, sell, sell.' I'll have to worm my way into her affections by buying something. If you can cut off eighths, that would be fine."

"You found a designer?"

"No problem there, and I've got the right girl."

Sandy felt stupidly disappointed.

"She's perfect," he said enthusiastically. "Marvelous face and figure, a fine dancer, and quite a pretty voice."

Sandy got very busy cutting the strips of fabric, bending over the job so he could not see her face. She felt stupid. The man had mentioned right off that he was shopping for a special girl. Now he had her safe and sound, and she was a lovely creature with all sorts of talents. So what!

"She hasn't had much experience," the young man was saying, dreamily watching Sandy's hands. "That might turn out to be an advantage in a lot of ways. I can teach her what she needs to know, and I won't have to break her of a lot of bad habits."

Sandy almost dropped her scissors out of sheer indignation. Never had she heard anything so outrageously smug and sexist. And to think she had actually taken a liking to the man!

He was staring at the bolts of fabric and didn't notice her reaction. "We'll definitely have to do something about her hair," he went on in the same thoughtful tone. "She had it dyed black for her last gig, and it sticks up and out like a brush. She looks more like a porcupine than a juvenile lead."

Something strange happened to Sandy's stomach. It simply flipped over. The room tilted for a moment, then straightened up and settled back where it belonged. She suddenly felt very happy. "I'm glad she decided to audition for you," she said shyly. "I knew she was thinking about it. And she really is very lovely, although she hasn't done any legit work."

The young man looked surprised, then delighted.

Sandy suddenly realized what she was saying and finished up lamely, "Well, that was my understanding."

"You know Deb? What a coincidence. Small world and all that."

"I only overheard her talking to a friend," Sandy mumbled, terribly embarrassed. "I just happened to be nearby. I don't really know her."

"I've been to parties like that. All the best conversations are going on somewhere else, while you're pinned to the wall by a monumental bore who insists on telling you about last season's baseball scores. Well, if you've seen Deb, then you know what we have to work with. Did she tell you about the play?"

Sandy shook her head.

"It's another version of the Cinderella story," he explained eagerly. "Only it's set in Washington, D.C., in an election year. The Cinderella character works for this senator. . . . Listen, I'd like to talk to you about it. Will you have lunch with me?"

Sandy decided that for once she would not work through her lunch hour. "I get off at twelve," she said, "but I have only half an hour."

"I'll grab some fast food for both of us, and we can eat at one of those tables overlooking the fountain. Okay?"

Sandy nodded.

"I'll be back then." He took the bundle of fabric from her and held her hand for a moment.

"Perhaps I'd better introduce myself. My name's Jason Grant."

"I knew it was Jason," she said, smiling.

They sat at a tiny table, overlooking not only the fountain, but the whole orderly confusion of ramps, stairways, and escalators that connected the different levels of the mall.

"Monstrous, isn't it?" Jason said. "If Piranesi had designed stage sets, they would have looked just like that."

"I saw an old movie the other night," Sandy said dreamily. "There were miles of stairs, not going anywhere in particular, just stairs for the sake of stairs, and women in marvelous costumes—at least the headdresses were wonderful—slowly walking up and down to music. I don't think there was any plot."

"Stairs are good," he agreed. "I wish we had a bigger stage to work with, but we ought to be able to manage at least three or four shallow steps for the ballroom scene. You see, our problem is we don't have the facilities for a professional production."

"Semiprofessional isn't so bad," Sandy suggested helpfully. "After all, you're using amateurs only for the supporting parts."

He looked pleased. "We don't need a big cast. The author wrote in a lot of action that does nothing for the play. It's never been done by professionals, you see. So he put in a lot of bit parts

and crowd scenes, just to oblige all those amateurs yearning for their moment of glory, and to
dress up the set. I've cut all that. A tape offstage
gives us the feel of the crowd, that and the light
streaming through a doorway. The focus is on
the people and what they're saying. It stops being
a show and becomes a play. What do you think?"

"I don't know a thing about plays," Sandy admitted. "I listened in on a conversation, that's
all. I think I got myself invited to lunch on false
pretenses."

"Are you trying to tell me that you suckered
me into buying you this perfectly delicious hamburger—not to mention the limp French fries—
by pretending to be a theater person?" He was
laughing at her. "Miss Sandra Childs, I am
shocked and grieved."

"I listened to your Cinderella girl and another
woman, and it sounded so interesting." Sandy
was thoroughly embarrassed. "I didn't mean to
give you the impression that I'm a theater person—well, maybe I did. I got so fascinated. I
wanted to hear more about it."

"I have seldom been so flattered," Jason said,
grinning. "Sandra, isn't it?"

"Sandy."

"Okay, Sandy. You have just been promoted
from theater person to audience substitute. Let
me give you the background of this production.
The place where I work has an auditorium that
gets used only once or twice a month for fashion

shows, meetings, stuff like that. The rest of the time it sits there and gathers dust. So I've persuaded the boss to let me use it for an amateur theater group. Last fall we put on Noel Coward's *Tonight at 8:30* with astounding success, considering that we're just a bunch of amateurs."

"You directed a professional summer theater," Sandy protested. "You were very good."

"So I was," he agreed, pleased. "For a non-theater person you're well-informed. I'm quite a competent director, not to mention a fair character actor. So there we were, having made a good start, with no place to go but up and out. We decided to tackle something bigger, and here we are."

"And you have professional actors working for you." Sandy's enthusiasm was dampened by a new thought. "Now you'll have to come up with big sets and costumes and music and all that."

"Big sets would be nice," Jason agreed wistfully. "What I have is a tiny stage that has to work like a big one. Listen, Sandy, are you just being nice, or are you really interested?"

"I'm hooked," she admitted.

"Then you must come and look at our setup," he said eagerly. "When do you get through tonight?"

Sandy was doubtful. "We usually close up by six-thirty, but I don't know. . . ."

Jason became brisk and efficient. "Should I

pick you up here or at your place? Do you have a car here that you want to take home first?"

"My roommate does the driving." Sandy felt pleasantly confused. "We could go straight to your theater from here, as long as I tell her not to wait for me."

"Fine," Jason said, gathering up the debris from their lunch and stacking it on the tray. "I'll toss the trash. You'd better step on it, or the sell-sell lady will have heart failure. Does she have a heart? Never mind. I don't want to know. I'll come back for you. Be a pal and wait if I should happen to be a few minutes late. I have some running around to do before we can get away."

She watched him loping off and sideswiping more leisurely shoppers. He was the oddest man Sandy had ever met. He was a complete stranger, and a broken-down actor at that. She had no business making a date with him, but she felt breathlessly, idiotically happy.

Chapter Four

*T*HEY took a bus from the mall to Public
Square, only a few blocks from the old ware-
house district.

"I prefer public transportation," Jason explained. "It's more convenient than using a car.
By the time you've found a parking place. . . .
And afterward there's always the problem of
finding where you left it and extricating yourself."

Sandy had a flash of insight into her companion. Obviously he couldn't admit that he didn't
own a car. She realized that he was sensitive
about his poverty and blessed herself for not having offered to pay for her hamburger. That would
have hurt his feelings. She did, however, promise
herself that the next time he offered to buy something for her, she would come up with some sort
of an excuse.

"We're almost there," he said, pulling her past
the imposing entrance of the Brae-Mill plant and
pointing down a dark alley. "It won't do for a

41

theater entrance, of course. The audience comes in through the reception area, which is carpeted and very plush. They even get to use the executive elevator. That one, I suspect, was designed by the original Mr. Otis himself. It has mirrors, lots of fancy brass fittings, and clap-down upholstered seats, believe it or not, so you can sit when you get stuck between floors. We, on the other hand, use the freight elevator, which has the advantage of seldom getting stuck. It's brand-new."

They soared smoothly to the top of the building and came out on a surprisingly elegant corridor, which was wide and deeply carpeted.

"Executive offices," Jason explained. "Mrs. Moffat's waiting for us in the conference room. We'll talk to her first, so she can get home. Then I'll show you the theater."

"Who's Mrs. Moffat?"

He grabbed her hand and hustled her along. "The designer I told you about. She won't let you call her that. It's a case of inverted snobbery. She's a cutter. If pushed, she might admit to doing the drafting and being a pattern maker, but that's as far as she'll bend. She's a staunch union member. You'll like her."

Mrs. Moffat was waiting for them. She had a strong, square face, untidy gray hair, kind eyes, and the most wonderful hands Sandy had ever seen. They were square and powerful, and she moved them decisively. Sandy felt those hands told more about Mrs. Moffat than her words or facial expression ever could.

"You're late," she said crisply. "Did you bring the swatches?"

"Swatches," he said, spilling the contents of his knapsack onto the big table. "I also went to the library and ran off copies of a whole bunch of stuff about social functions, gowns worn by first ladies. I looked at stills from *Gone with the Wind* and resisted the temptation. We don't want to copy."

"Nothing wrong with copying something good," Mrs. Moffat said calmly.

"And I brought Sandy Childs, who's interested in theater."

Mrs. Moffat produced a harrumphing sound that indicated complete lack of enthusiasm.

"She understands fabric," Jason added.

For the first time, Mrs. Moffat actually looked at Sandy. "Interested in textiles?" she demanded. "Hand weaving? Wholesale production? Design?"

"I would like to design clothes," Sandy said humbly. "Jason said you're a very good cutter."

Mrs. Moffat's eyes smiled and her hands reached out and grabbed Sandy's. It was a strange sensation. Mrs. Moffat's fingertips seemed to read the bones and muscles of Sandy's hands, turning them this way and that, and giving them an approving pat before letting go.

Sandy had an odd feeling that Mrs. Moffat now knew more about her than she did herself.

"Well?" Mrs. Moffat demanded. "Which one of these fabrics do you like best?"

Sandy's fingers hovered over the tangle of swatches. Slowly she separated them, arranged them in a pattern that made sense to her, and picked out a glowing, iridescent taffeta, red of course, but with peach highlights and lilac shadows.

Mrs. Moffat gave a grunt of approval. "I like that one too. Now, what would you do with it?"

She pushed a drawing pad and a pencil across the table at Sandy as Jason pulled out a chair. For a moment Sandy stared at the blank paper. Then her fingers tightened around the pencil and she began to draw. The figure had no head. There was only the slope of the shoulders, the nipped-in waist, and the bell shape of the skirt. She paused, closing her eyes to get a better view of Cinderella in her shimmering red gown. Suddenly it came to her. Of course, that was it: a plain neckline, cut straight across just below the collarbone to the very edge of the shoulder. Not a low-cut bodice at all—that had been the wrong idea. Now ideas came flying into Sandy's head.

Within minutes her creation was complete— and it looked darn good, she had to admit.

"Is that it?" Jason sounded excited. "There also has to be some sort of wrap. She enters at the top of the stairs—remember we talked about the stairs?—and she should drop some outer garment, just cast it off. I'd like her to have a cape or a scarf, something she can unfasten with both hands raised to her shoulders, and flick backward without looking. I just see that movement in my head."

Sandy thought for a moment, then reached for the drawing pad again. Not exactly a cloak or a scarf. It had to be something very bulky but weightless.

"Tulle," she said. "A lighter color than the dress, either pink or lilac, and gathered—like this." Her pencil flew over the surface of the pad. "Like smocking, only on a larger scale, so you have this airy, puffed look. That would look nice as it falls away from her. It shouldn't really fall, but sort of float to the ground. It could be held by a satin band across the front." She frowned thoughtfully. "If she puts up her hands to her shoulders, she can unhook the right corner, hold the wrap in both hands for a moment, and then flick it away as she steps forward. Is that what you had in mind?"

"That's it." Jason looked enormously pleased. "How did you know?" He turned to Mrs. Moffat almost accusingly. "I had no idea she had it in her. How come you guessed?"

"Her hands," Mrs. Moffat said simply. "She has good hands. But the poor girl knows nothing, nothing at all." She bent over Sandy's drawing. "Look here. You show fullness here and here, but how do you control it, eh? Do you want godets? Darts? Pleats? Gathers?"

"Not pleats, and certainly not gathers." Sandy chewed on the end of the pencil. "It should be as smooth as possible. What's a godet?"

"A bias insert." Mrs. Moffat grunted thoughtfully. "If we cut the whole dress on the bias. . . . Yes, I think that might work. Do you know how to turn a drawing into a pattern?"

Sandy numbly shook her head.

"Do you want to learn?"

Sandy nodded, almost afraid to breathe.

"Hmm—I'll have to talk to Mr. Miller. He's been after me for years to train someone, but the girls they send me are useless. The last one didn't want to be a cutter at all. She wanted to model; that's what she's doing in New York, and she's earning fifty times what she would have made as a trainee. But you want to learn, don't you?"

Sandy merely nodded.

Mrs. Moffat's hands did some figuring. "You'd better give notice at whatever job you have right now. I'll want you full-time. You'd best come in tomorrow, when the office is open, after nine. Go to Personnel and fill out the forms. I don't know what they'll offer you in the way of wages. I started at thirty-five dollars a week. I was sixteen at the time, and I thought I was lucky." She smiled. "I think they'll do a bit better for you. The union's not been sitting on its hands."

"I've saved up a bit," Sandy offered eagerly. "I could work without pay for a while."

"Don't you dare," Mrs. Moffat said. "Don't put ideas in their heads. Management will take advantage of you if you let them. Ask Jason. He can tell you a few things."

She nodded at them and went out, taking the swatches and the drawing pad with her.

"Isn't she terrific?" Jason asked. "I knew she'd take to you, even though I had no idea you were looking for a job. But I should have known. You're wasted where you are."

"It's all I was able to get," Sandy explained. "I come from Pottersville. I don't suppose you've heard of it. It doesn't show up too well on the map. It's the small dot that always gets folded into the creases. Lots of opportunities in Pottersville: the china works or—if you prefer—the china works. I emptied the piggy bank to come to Cleveland, hoping to wangle my way into an art school."

"You've come to a better place," Jason assured her. "Mrs. Moffat knows all there is to know about pattern making and she'll teach you. I've known her all my life, and she is the kindest, the most generous. . . . You see, my parents died when I was quite small, and she's been a sort of mother substitute to me."

Several puzzle pieces now fell into place. So that was why a would-be actor had come to work for Brae-Mill. Mrs. Moffat had managed to arrange the job for him, the same way she was making room for Sandy. Of course! That explained everything.

The auditorium was an elegant room, deeply carpeted in a deep, rich brown. Ranks of folding chairs were stacked against the walls. Not the plain, slatted variety, these were finished in black lacquer and upholstered in leather. The stage, on the other hand, was a disappointment; it was really no more than a shallow alcove raised three feet above the floor, framed by brown velvet curtains, and backed by a folding screen of pleated, creamy material. Steps curved down either side of the stage, and a platform jutted into the room, ending in a tablelike arrangement in the middle, under the chandelier.

"Right now it looks worse than it is," Jason explained. "We put on a fashion show a couple of days ago. The walkway goes, and the screen. The stage isn't really that small, just too small for what I would like to do." He held out his hand. "Come and look at the back."

Sandy admired the sweep of the stage behind the screen, the dressing rooms, and the banks of lights overhead.

"In a real theater," Jason explained wistfully, "that would be the flies. You'd have the various backdrops up there ready to be lowered into place, and banks of lights." He shrugged. "Well, this is what we have to work with, and it's not

as bad as you might think. We have better work-
shops than most of the small houses, and a sup-
ply of props that can't be beat."

"Props?"

"Properties, Sandy, bits and pieces you need
onstage. Haven't you ever done a play? Not even
in school?"

"There used to be a Pottersville Drama Club,"
Sandy admitted sadly, "but it folded before I got
into high school, and anyway I don't think my
parents would have approved."

"I know." Jason pulled a solemn face, then
burst into song. " 'Life upon the wicked stage is
nothing for a girl.' "

Sandy giggled, then protested, "It wasn't really like that. They have nothing against the theater. It's just that they wanted me to spend more
time out-of-doors. They worried about my taking up a lot of hobbies that kept me away from
fresh air, so they pushed sports. My brothers are
jocks, all three of them, so I guess it seemed un-
natural to Mom and Dad that I'd want to sit
around sewing and drawing."

"Neurotic," Jason agreed. "So you have three
brothers, all ten feet tall and bulging with muscle. Any sisters?"

"I'm the only girl, and they're nice, ordinary
guys, not muscle-bound freaks."

"I'm sorry." He grinned and threw his arm
around her shoulders. "It's sheer envy on my
side. I'm an only child, and my grandfather's not

a family-minded sort of person. He's not a bad guy, but I don't think it ever occurred to him to wonder whether I stayed indoors or went swimming in the middle of winter. I've always thought what fun it must be to belong to one of those close-knit families that take a real interest in each other. Yours sounds great."

"They are," Sandy agreed. "But it can get a bit suffocating. They take such an intense interest in every single thing I do. It's nice of them to care, but. . . ."

"It sounds good to me," Jason insisted. "You'll get no sympathy from me on the basis of having a family who cares what happens to you. Now, you've seen my playground, so it's time to look for a place to eat. That's one thing I've found out about women. You have to feed them at regular intervals. If you don't, they begin to droop, and I need to keep you in good condition. Otherwise we won't get any work out of you. Do you like Greek food?"

"I'm not a bit hungry," Sandy protested hastily. "Really, I'm not."

He consulted his watch. "It's after eight. If you're not hungry by now, that means your stomach has given up hope and has gone into a holding pattern. If we don't feed you soon, you will turn faint and do something lovely and Victorian, like swooning. Has it occurred to you that a man may occasionally faint from pain or fatigue, but women have the option of swooning instead? It's one of those sexist privileges, utterly unfair. Do stop standing there glaring at me. If you think I'm a chauvinist pig, tell me about it. Hit me over the head or something, but do come along."

Sandy allowed herself to be dragged along. She had never come up against this particular form of persuasion. Jason talked as if he were bent on having his own way, but she felt that it was just a facade, to cover up the concern he had for other people. He was, she decided, the nicest man she had ever met.

She was determined not to let him spend a lot of money on her, to order the cheapest thing on the menu, but she was given no opportunity to order anything, cheap or otherwise. The counterman at the all-night diner offered no menu. Instead, he spread his arms wide and shouted a noisy welcome: "Hey, Jason, you late! What's the matter with you? Worried about your waistline?"

"Hi, Joe," Jason responded with a grin. "What's good tonight?"

Joe had a glossy, suntanned head and a thick accent. "Just soup," he announced. "At least it's real soup, not from can. I make it myself, chicken backs, eggs, and fresh lemon juice, very good."

"Avgolemono soup? Great! We'll start with that."

When the bowls were set before them, Sandy

inhaled the rich fragrance of the soup and realized how hungry she really was. Jason started to eat, while continuing the discussion. "What else you got?"

"Not much," Joe protested. "You come in too late. We had a nice spinach pie, but that's all gone, and *dolmadakia, keftaides,* and *loukanika,* a lovely *stefado,* all gone."

"Not to worry," Jason reassured him. "I trust you. You won't let us starve. We can eat ham and eggs, if you've got nothing else."

"Well, I could fry you up some kalamaria," Joe admitted.

Jason turned to Sandy. "Joe never lets me down. He's the best cook in town and a mother hen at heart. He really likes feeding people."

"But the soup's very filling," Sandy protested. "I don't think I want anything else."

"Baloney," Jason said brusquely. "Joe's kalamaria deserve your attention. You like fish, don't you?"

Sandy nodded, feeling rather befuddled by the way Jason jumped from one subject to the next.

"Well, if you like fish, you'll adore kalamaria. They're little baby squid, breaded and fried, as only Joe can fry them."

Sandy gave in. It was easier than trying to argue with Jason. Her only comfort was that the diner looked inexpensive, and Joe seemed to be a friend, unlikely to charge too much. They ate the squid and a salad, drank wonderful black coffee, and finished up with a pastry of decadent opulence.

"Nothing fills up those cracks like a piece of baklava," Jason said, patting his midriff. "Thank you, Joe. You've done it again."

To Sandy's horror, he tossed two twenty-dollar bills onto the counter and grabbed her arm.

"Wait for your change," she hissed.

He looked down at her with surprise, then grinned. "But I eat here all the time. I'm sure Joe keeps a running tab."

She had to be content with that, although it worried her that he should be so careless with money.

"And now we have to get you home," he said when they got out into the dark street. "This is one of those times when one would like to magic up a car."

"We're close to Public Square," Sandy said quickly. "I can catch a bus from there. The 7a runs all night and goes within four blocks of where I live."

"You intend to walk?"

"Of course. Why not? I like walking."

"Late at night—probably through a high-crime area? Lady, you're not quite right in the head." But he laughed as he said it and fell into step beside her.

Without quite knowing how it had happened, Sandy found that he had his arm around her waist and hers was hugging his scratchy sweater. It was warm and pleasant walking like that.

The Square was bleakly still under its brilliant lights. The only movement was the mess of papers twirling in front of the Terminal Tower Building.

"Have you ever noticed that this spot always has a miniature twister?" Jason marveled. "Even when it's dead calm everywhere else. There's no bus, of course, never is when you want one."

"It'll be along soon," Sandy assured him. "I'm sure it will. They run every half hour. I'll wait."

"Poor thinking," Jason decided. "But, not to worry. I see a taxi. Let's try to wake up the driver."

"Don't." Sandy was horrified. "I live in Cleveland Heights. It would cost a fortune."

He ignored her protests and dragged her to the cab, opened the door, and pushed her inside.

"But I want to wait for the bus," she wailed. "Let me out of here."

Jason leaned against the door to keep it closed, and addressed himself to the yawning cabbie.

"The poor girl's overwrought," he explained cheerfully. "Take her home. She'll give you the address as soon as she calms down a bit. Don't let her stray off by herself." To Sandy's horror, he handed over another twenty. "Keep the change."

The cab pulled away from the curb before

Sandy had a chance to grab the money and jump out.

"You been having a fight?" the driver inquired. "Your friend's real eager to get rid of you."

"He has no business spending so much money on me." Sandy was almost in tears. "He can't afford it."

"Some women are forever trying to run a man's life," the cabbie observed with a shrug. "Why don't you let the guy decide what he wants to spend his money on? There's nothing worse than a bossy female. I used to date a girl who worried over every penny I spent, from the extra cheese on the pizza to the quarter I put in the jukebox. She was a good-looking dame, cute as a button, but she got to be a real pain. Don't act that way, lady, not if you want to hang on to your fella. Now, where did you say you were going?"

Chapter Five

*M*RS. Roberts was outraged when Sandy not only gave two weeks' notice, but asked for a couple of hours off in the same breath.

"And what am I supposed to do while you are gallivanting around town? I can't sell and keep an eye on the shop at the same time."

"I'll be back before lunch. It doesn't usually get busy till then." Sandy felt sorry for the old woman with her stiff, pink hair and her frightened little eyes. "I'll hurry as much as I can."

"There's no such thing as loyalty to a job these days," Mrs. Roberts snapped ungraciously. "Here today and gone tomorrow. I thought you were settling in nicely. I was even thinking of giving you a raise."

The personnel department at Brae-Mill had all the intimate charm of an assembly line. Sandy filled out a great many forms and was finally interviewed by a man whose nostrils appeared to be permanently pinched in disgust. He seemed so bored by the interview that Sandy found herself fighting off a yawning fit. Boredom, she discovered, is catching. When the interview was concluded, however, and the personnel manager had given his last fastidious sniff, Sandy had a card that identified her as a bona fide employee of the Brae-Mill Company, and the personnel department had a folder with a great deal of information concerning Sandra Childs. It also contained Sandra Childs's signature, certifying that all this information was indeed true to the best of her knowledge, and that she promised to work at five dollars an hour for a period of three months, her salary to be renegotiated at that time on the basis of her performance.

On her way out, Sandy bumped into Pete. She knew she'd run into him eventually, since he worked there, but she'd hoped it wouldn't be quite this soon.

"You're looking for me," he said hopefully. "You should have told them at the front desk. The receptionist would have called me."

Sandy quickly explained that she had come to apply for a job, and was in fact starting work in two weeks.

"That's terrific!" Pete was immensely pleased. "Then we'll be able to have lunch together in the cafeteria, and I can drive you to and from work. It'll save you bus fares."

"My hours may be a bit irregular," Sandy explained, edging away from him. "It's not an office job. I'm starting as a trainee in drafting. Mrs. Moffat seems to work all hours, so I guess I will too."

"Mrs. Moffat presumes on her position in the firm," Pete said, frowning. "She's been here for so long, I sometimes think she feels she owns the company." He became increasingly indignant as he thought about it. "Don't let her take advantage of you, Sandy. You'll have to stand up for yourself."

Sandy was glad to get away from him. She hoped the bookkeeping department and Mrs. Moffat's workshop were separated by miles and miles of corridor.

"A new job?" Meg said. "Hey, things are looking up. First you dump Pete the Pro, and now you're doing something to further your career. How much does it pay?"

"Five dollars an hour for the first three months."

Meg groaned. "I don't believe you, kid. You're not real. How can you change a bad job for one that's even worse? You pay out more than that for your share of the rent, groceries, and the car."

"I won't be paying you for gas anymore." Sandy was apologetic. "Brae-Mill's downtown, so I'll be taking the bus. As for the rent and all that, I'll just dig into my savings. I can hold out for three months, and then—"

"By then they'll know they've got a sucker," Meg said bitterly. "They'll never pay you a decent salary, not once they've got you safe and sound, and have you psyched out. You're such a sap."

"I know," Sandy admitted. "It doesn't sound practical, but it is the chance I've been waiting for. I'll be learning the trade, you see. At last I'm really going to learn something."

Meg sighed. "You're hopeless, but I can't let you starve. Forget the food money. The eats will be on me. Just pay your half of the rent for the next three months. And if they refuse to give you a decent raise at that time, I shall personally go down to the Brae-Mill payroll department and push someone's teeth down someone's throat."

"It's nice to have friends," Sandy said, grinning.

It was a good thing Sandy had a sweet temper. Her last two weeks at Sew Nice would have tried a less amiable disposition. Mrs. Roberts was grimly determined to get her money's worth from an employee selfish enough to go out and find a better job. The old lady's temper was not improved by the difficulties she encountered when she tried to find a saleswoman who would do what Sandy had done without complaint.

"From nine to six-thirty, no regular lunch hour, and no overtime paid for staying late?" one applicant said, picking up her bag. "Lady, don't you know that slavery's no longer legal?"

The next applicant was more polite. "I would consider the job, except for the late evenings. My husband works nights, and I have to be home to take care of the children before he has to leave."

Polite or not, they all said no.

"I can't possibly take such a cut in salary. If you could raise the wage you are offering by two dollars an hour. . . ."

"I love selling, but I'm afraid I can't take on a job that won't let me sit down at least part of the time. My arches, you know. . . ."

Mrs. Roberts was frustrated and panic-stricken. She had forgotten how difficult life had been before Sandy's arrival.

"I can't let you go," she decided angrily. "You'll just have to stay on until we find the right girl."

Sandy spent her supposed lunch hour calling several employment agencies, and two days later, the problem was solved. What Mrs. Roberts needed was not one, but two saleswomen. Mrs. Clay was to arrive at nine, open up, and work until one. This allowed her to be home before her children got out of school. Miss Novak, who was taking a morning class at Community College, checked in at one-thirty and stayed until closing time.

"That still leaves me alone in the middle of the day," Mrs. Roberts complained. "It just won't do. You'll have to stay until something better turns up."

There is a point when even a saintly temper boils over. Sandy was gentler than most people would have been.

"I'm very sorry," she said firmly. "I've done all I can, and I'm starting my new job Monday morning. I hope things will work out for you. Good-bye."

"Ungrateful!" Mrs. Roberts shrilled after her. "Disloyal! You won't go far with that sort of attitude. You'll see. Don't say I didn't warn you."

"Well, that takes care of the Wicked Witch of the West," Meg said, driving Sandy home from the mall for the last time. "Want to come out with Al and me tonight to celebrate your escape?"

Sandy smilingly shook her head.

"I need to zonk out," she said, but the thought came unbidden into her mind that she would have gone, however tired, if Jason would make it a foursome.

Monday morning found Sandy part of the stream of workers converging on the Brae-Mill block. She had carefully picked an outfit worthy of her new career. The dark plaid dress with its spotless white collar and cuffs was not as good as a tailored suit, but it did look cool and competent. With it, Sandy was wearing the high-heeled boots of soft, crushed leather that had made such a hole in her budget. Instead of a shoulder bag, she carried a briefcase, borrowed from Meg. Sandy felt she looked experienced and serious.

It was also a very becoming outfit. There was, after all, a good chance that she would be bumping into Jason from time to time. The red velvet ribbon under the collar was for him.

She followed the other workers through the side door, where they lined up at the clock. Waiting until everyone had punched in, she searched for a card with her name on it but couldn't find one. A latecomer came rushing in and almost knocked her down.

"Move over!" the girl yelled, hastily pushing her card into the slot. "Whew, I just made it. They docked me half an hour last week, when I was only one minute late. I'm going to take that up with the union. It's not fair. I clock in several minutes early most of the time. Have they given you the same runaround?"

"I suppose they will. It's my first day, and I can't even find my card."

"If they haven't given you a card, they can't dock you for being late," the girl shouted over her shoulder, hurrying down the corridor. "Lucky you."

Sandy stood by the clock, wondering what she was supposed to do, when Mrs. Moffat stepped out of the elevator.

"So here you are. I rather thought this might

happen. They should have told you in personnel. You won't be punching the clock. There'd be no sense in it. You'll be working late a good part of the time." She took in Sandy's elegant outfit. "Why are you dressed for the front office? You can't work in those clothes."

Sandy felt silly. Mrs. Moffat wore a gray lab coat, the pockets bulging with pencils, rulers, and other tools of her craft. Her hair was tucked under a drab scarf, and her feet were decked out in shapeless but comfortable-looking shoes. Compared to that practical outfit, Sandy's clothes were ridiculous.

"Never mind," Mrs. Moffat said kindly. "This way you'll make a nice impression. I was going to give you the tour of the plant later this week, but they had better see you today in all your splendor. Once you've been looked over, you'll be able to frump around with the rest of us."

"I'd like to see the plant. If you have time."

"I don't really," Mrs. Moffat admitted. "But I'd better do it myself, or they'll fill your ears with a lot of nonsense. We'll start at the top, because that's where the whole process gets started, in my drafting room."

"Where I met you?"

Mrs. Moffat laughed heartily. "A very different part of the same floor. Mr. Miller and the top executives have their offices in front, and the back is drafting and development, and the sample room, of course."

The elevator took them to the carpeted corridor she remembered, but they turned right instead of left, and came into a brightly lit, linoleum-floored passage.

"This looks like a factory." Sandy was surprised by the abrupt change.

"This is a factory. I'll give you a quick look at my room. I like open shelves, because I tend to lose things. Miss Crocker says it makes for dust, but most of these things don't stay long enough to gather dust."

Sandy admired the big worktable, the adjustable draftboard, and the carpeted platform in the middle of the room.

"We don't use that so much these days," Mrs. Moffat said wistfully. "I'd rather drape than draft. I like to work on a model—some people use a fitting form, but I never did. You drape the fabric and pin it on the model, and then you trace the cutting pattern from the draped sections. It's the old-fashioned way, and still the best in my opinion, but it takes time."

They went next door and met Miss Crocker, who didn't like open shelves. Miss Crocker was a severe-looking woman. Her lab coat looked crisper than Mrs. Moffat's, and her hair was sternly confined in a net. She was bent over a machine and ignored her visitors.

"Miss Crocker has been grading almost as long as I have been cutting." Mrs. Moffat was smiling at the other woman's tense back.

"Grading?" Sandy asked doubtfully. "Like trimming seams in layers?"

Miss Crocker snorted disdainfully, and Mrs. Moffat laughed.

"Don't look now but your amateur status is hanging out. Grading is the fine art of adjusting the pattern to all the different sizes without changing the style. Miss Crocker got started long before they published the anthropometric tables. Grading really was an art in those days."

"Never an art," Miss Crocker snapped over her shoulder. "It was a science then as it is now. We just used our heads instead of the tables."

"The first machines came in about the time you were born, Sandy," Mrs. Moffat explained. "Now it's all computerized, and Anne Crocker is still the best grader in the business."

Miss Crocker actually looked up and smiled, then turned her back on them again. Taking the hint, they tiptoed out.

"Cutting room next?" Sandy asked eagerly.

"Not quite. We have another important department up here, the sample room. We'll just stick our heads through the door. These are the people you will be working with a good part of the time. It's like a dressmaking shop, at least the way they used to look. This is where we run up samples. You can't go into production until the sample has been approved."

They put their heads in the door, waved at the three women working there, and went on.

"Now," Mrs. Moffat said, "we will pretend that we have one of Miss Crocker's cutting patterns in this cart, and we'll take it down to the next floor."

"To the cutting room?"

"Be patient. How long do you think our pattern would last if we laid it out by hand, and how much fabric do you think we would waste? All these pattern pieces must be photographed and reduced in size. Then they're arranged for layout economy, and the marking paper is printed up. That's what goes on top of the fabric."

The marking process was interesting, but Sandy yearned to see the actual cutting.

"It's not what you expect," Mrs. Moffat warned her. "Here's a finished marking pattern. Looks like the sheet of tissue paper you take from an envelope at home, doesn't it?"

It did look familiar, except for the scale. This was not one sheet of thin paper, but a huge roll.

As they were following the cart with the marking pattern down the hallway, Jason suddenly dashed from an elevator and grabbed Sandy's hand.

"You add class to this place," he shouted, his eyes warm and approving on the red velvet bow. "Do you think you'll like it?"

Sandy nodded enthusiastically. "It's wonderful."

"Take care," he warned her, grinning. "This

outfit will drain the lifeblood out of you, if you let them. Protect yourself. Join the union."

"She already has," Mrs. Moffat reminded him tartly. "This is a union shop, and a good thing too."

Jason broke into song. " 'There once was a union maid. . . .' "

"Go away and play somewhere else," Mrs. Moffat protested. "We don't have time for your nonsense."

" '. . . who never was afraid . . .' " Jason went on singing, striding along between Sandy and Mrs. Moffat, one arm flung around each of their waists. " '. . . of goons and ginks and company finks. . . .' "

Mrs. Moffat surprisingly joined in: " '. . . and Pinkerton men who make the raid.' " She extricated herself from Jason's arm. "Now run along, Jason, there's a good boy. We have work to do."

"True, we are all wage slaves around here." Jason gave Sandy's waist a last quick squeeze before letting go. "Just remember, you have the union behind you in all its awful majesty. Don't let them push you around."

He waved his hand cheerfully and dodged into one of the exits. Mrs. Moffat was laughing.

"Back to the real world," she said. "Cutting room next."

Sandy was quivering with excitement. This was what she had been waiting for—and Jason had noticed the ribbon. Maybe he knew that that was for him, just as the rest of her outfit was for Brae-Mill.

The actual cutting room, however, was sobering, not at all what Sandy had expected. She had been looking for cutting tables, but this room was dominated by monstrous machines carrying bolts of fabric back and forth, spreading layer upon layer of fabric. They stopped only briefly at each end, clicking as they made the end cut, then continuing on their journey.

"Perfect each trip," Mrs. Moffat explained proudly. "The pattern goes on top, fastened down with two-sided tape, and then you're ready for cutting." She regarded the monsters with affection. "When I think of the old turntable spreader we had when I started! Mr. Miller got it secondhand and it was forever breaking down."

Sandy watched amazed as the machine deposited more and more layers of cloth, picking up new bolts as it went.

"How are they going to cut through those piles of cloth?" she asked.

Mrs. Moffat laughed. "Not with scissors, I can tell you that. Not even with a rotary blade, which is what I used when I got started. That was hard work. I was thrilled when we installed the band knives, but they weren't foolproof, either. What we have now is all computerized—no blades at all, just a laser beam that goes through all these pattern lays like a hot knife through butter. I'll introduce you to Tracy before we move on. I see she's not busy."

Tracy was a very young girl, butter-blond and stunning even in her shapeless coveralls.

"My notcher is down again," she greeted them mournfully. "Mr. Hicks thinks I did something to it, but I just don't understand machines."

"At least you know you won't get fired," Mrs. Moffat assured her, then turned to Sandy to explain. "Tracy's our best model, a perfect size eight. You'd never guess how few people come in standard sizes. Tracy has job security. She's worth her weight in gold—as long as she holds that weight."

Tracy pulled a face. "I have to be careful not to gain weight, or to lose it, or to put on too much muscle, or to let my muscles sag. My job's safe just as long as I don't change." She sighed. "I wish I understood machines. Then I'd have *real* job security."

"I'll see if we can't get you transferred to the sample room," Mrs. Moffat said. "You can run a sewing machine, can't you?"

They left Tracy glaring at her notcher and went down to the next floor.

"This is production," Mrs. Moffat announced, and Sandy knew she was indeed in a clothing factory.

The huge room roared with the sound of sewing machines; Mrs. Moffat had to shout to make herself heard above the din. Sandy strained her ears as Mrs. Moffat explained the functions of all the different machines and their attachments. She spoke of feed systems, tension adjustments, templets, seam folders, binders, thread trimmers, needle positioners, and stackers. Sandy found the latter rather frightening. They practically grabbed the work away from the operators and moved them along to the next work station.

"How do they stand it?" Sandy demanded.

Mrs. Moffat understood. "It's hard, though not as bad as it used to be. The noise is the worst, that and working against the clock."

"And when something comes out of here, it's completely finished," Sandy marveled. "I thought there would be other rooms, where they trimmed away the threads and sewed on buttons, stuff like that."

"All that's left now is pressing and forming," Mrs. Moffat agreed. "We won't go into the pressing rooms. It's all done with buck presses these days. You've seen their little brothers at the dry cleaners. The curing chambers are interesting, but I just hate the smell. It makes me sick."

"Curing chambers?" asked Sandy. "Like slabs of bacon?"

"Not exactly. That's where they set the shape of some garments, like that seamless bra you're probably wearing. After that it's packing and shipping, and you've seen the offices—personnel, payroll, bookkeeping, purchasing, and sales. The cafeteria's in the basement."

"But I thought the offices were upstairs."

"Only the top executives have their offices on our floor. Let's get back. You've probably seen enough for one day."

Sandy was relieved to be back on the top floor. It had been a rather overwhelming experience. She spent the rest of the day in the sample room, manning a sewing machine, clipping threads, and sweeping the floor. She ended up at the ironing board, trying to coax the wrinkles out of a pile of ruffled shirts.

By five o'clock, a sharp pain had permanently settled in her lower back, and the beautiful plaid dress, which had been so immaculate, was covered with lint. Perhaps it was just as well that Jason had not come by their room and seen her looking like t' ,, but Sandy was disappointed all the same.

Mrs. Moffat observed Sandy's woebegone expression and understood at least part of the problem. "You won't last long if you don't learn to pace yourself," she advised. "Tomorrow you get here after the big rush is over, and you come properly dressed. You'll spend the morning with me. We'll get you started on the basics of drafting. In the afternoon you'll be working in samples again."

Sandy pushed both hands against her aching back and smiled. "I've never spent such a wonderful day. I had no idea there was so much to learn."

Mrs. Moffat nodded. "I'll give you a list of books you should be reading. If you can't get them from the library, I'll lend you my own copies. A lot of the stuff they would spoon-feed you at the Art Institute is yours for the taking, if you care to open the covers of a book. The rest I can teach you better myself, the same way I learned it, hands-on. Go home and soak in a hot bath for a while. Throw in a handful of Epsom salts, if you have them in the house. If your back still hurts after that, hook your fingers on the top of a doorframe and let yourself dangle for a while. I do it every night of my life."

Meg was astonished to see Sandy hanging by her fingertips in the doorway.

"Training for a Tarzan movie?" she suggested. "You Jane?"

Sandy slumped to the floor. "It's do-it-yourself traction, instant therapy for aching backs. Backs, I learned today, are the Achilles' heel of my chosen trade."

Meg kicked off her shoes and tried dangling. "Hey," she said, "this is neat. It really feels good. Maybe that's what's wrong with the human race: We basically belong back in the trees. Maybe I can persuade Al to take me to a nice quiet jungle someday, where we can swing from the branches and live on bananas."

Meg's way of bringing Al into every conversation had long been a puzzlement to Sandy. He seemed like a nice enough guy, more interesting than Pete but practically invisible when compared to someone really special—like Jason. Meg dated no one else.

"You really like Al, don't you?" Sandy said wistfully.

Meg turned pink and became elaborately off-hand. "He's pretty nice. I mean, he's okay. We have fun together." She sighed and became pensive. "I just wish he'd grow up. The trouble with men and women is that they don't mature at the same rate. When I started dating Al, we were kids, both of us. That worked out just fine. We had a ball. But now I seem to be growing up, and he still wants to play in the sandbox."

"He's not ready to make a commitment. Is that it?"

Meg picked up her shoes and threw them across the room. *"Commitment!* What a word. Honestly, Sandy, you come up with the dreariest expressions. I don't expect a solemn proposal on bended knee or an ironclad pledge of lifelong devotion. I just wish Al were a bit more serious."

"You made fun of poor old Pete because he was too serious," Sandy protested, "and now you blame Al for not being serious enough."

Meg frowned. "I just wish we'd spend more time sitting around, talking, stuff like that." She looked depressed. "He's such an airhead."

"But you're in love with him." Sandy couldn't imagine herself being in love with a man she didn't respect.

"Love's a funny business," Meg said with a sigh. "First time I met Al, he had acne and needed a haircut. I thought he was a nerd. And then his skin cleared up and he got a fancy set of wheels."

Sandy had to laugh. "You mean to tell me that you began to find him attractive as soon as he had a car?"

"Aren't cars supposed to be powerful sex symbols?" Meg asked doubtfully. "Maybe that has something to do with it. Anyway, he cut off enough hair so I finally got a look at his face. There was no one else just then, so I started going out with him, and after a while he began to grow on me."

"And now?"

Meg slumped down on the couch and linked her fingers behind her head. "Now I'm sort of hooked on him. That's what you have to watch out for. There's a point where a guy gets to you. One moment you're playing the field, having the time of your life, and all of a sudden all the other guys look sort of blah to you. It's not fair, but that's the way it is. You've got to avoid that. Don't be a sap like me. Make sure the man is serious about you before you get emotionally involved. If I'd played it cool with Al . . . and then again, maybe it wouldn't have made any difference."

She sounded so troubled that Sandy was concerned. "What's going to happen to you and Al? Will you get married someday?"

"I can only speak for myself," Meg said seriously. "I'm going to get married to someone. I hope it will be Al, because I really do love him. But if he won't grow up. . . . I suppose there might come a time when I have to cut my losses. I'm twenty-three. That's not so old. I can give it two more years."

"Wouldn't it be hard to give him up?"

Meg was staring up at the ceiling. "It would hurt." She sounded very sober. "But you have to have a game plan for your life. Mine is marriage—with Al if possible. If that doesn't work out . . . the game's still marriage."

Chapter Six

*S*andy was kept on the run. The job over-flowed into her spare time. She took to stopping off at the library on her way home, and she started reading the books Mrs. Moffat had listed. This craft she had chosen, she discovered, was more than making pretty pictures.

"Fashion drawings," Mrs. Moffat had snapped, sweeping a pile of Sandy's sketches into the wastebasket. "That's just presentation. It has nothing to do with the creation of a real garment. If that's what you like, get a job in advertising. Don't waste my time if all you want to do is make pretty pictures of people with ten-inch waists and giraffes' legs."

She saw Sandy's stricken face and became kind. "Look, what we do is something else. Fetch me that folder from the desk. Yes, that's the one. Look at this preliminary sketch for number 4218. You see, the structure has already been thought out. You can see that the shoulders are only moderately padded and that the sleeve is set in below the shoulder. What we were after was a soft, unstructured line. The color is indicated—only suggested, really—because nobody had looked at available fabrics at that point. That sketch was based on a design pirated from the West Coast."

"Stolen?" Sandy was rather shocked.

Mrs. Moffat shrugged. "That's the way it goes in the rag trade. We steal from them, and they steal from us. It's still only an idea. Now turn the page. See what I mean? That's what I did with that first sketch. It's not pretty, but the proportions are precise, and now you can see where every seam lies, as well as the direction of the nap. And I have taped swatches of possible fabric choices to the margin. Some of them have been circled. That means we considered those seriously. Keep going. This is one version that I wasted a lot of time on. I made up a muslin, and when it was tacked together, it just didn't work. That happens sometimes."

"It looks great," Sandy protested.

"Only on paper. There are some things you don't find out about a design until the model puts it on and walks around in it, raises her arms, sits down. That's the acid test. Now we get to the final version. The shoulders are still ever so slightly dropped, but they've changed. Can you see what we did?"

Sandy nodded. "I can see several changes. The shape of the armhole is different, slightly squared, and the seam has been turned the other way. And the lapels are narrower, aren't they?"

Mrs. Moffat was pleased with her pupil. "Small changes, big difference. We settled on the Dacron-and-wool blend, made our final decision on color, made up a line of samples, and arranged a trade show. I had my fingers crossed so tight, I still have the bruises to show. It paid off. Number 4218 was our best seller for two years."

"I remember that suit," Sandy said thoughtfully. "It was classy, only it wasn't wool. I tried it on at Higbee's last summer. It was denim."

"Everybody wore it. We made it up in denim, linen, corduroy, tweed, poplin, and ultrasuede for the carriage trade. Once you have a model that sells, you can run it up in different fabrics for different seasons and markets. No, don't put the book back on the shelf. It has to go down to Lisa Carnaby's office, though I can't think why she wants it. She's on the first floor, market research."

Unwilling to waste time waiting for the elevator, Sandy clattered down the stairs and arrived at Lisa Carnaby's office, flushed and somewhat out of breath. The moment she stepped through the door, she found herself wishing that she had taken time to comb her hair and splash cold water on her face.

"You must be Moffat's new gofer," Lisa Carnaby drawled, looking up from a desk as flawlessly tidy as she was herself. "Did you bring the number 4218?"

"Mrs. Moffat said you need it," Sandy stammered. "It's just a series of work drawings for a suit."

Miss Carnaby smiled. "For model 4218, I hope. Otherwise you are going to have to go all the way back and bring the right folder." She sounded cool and amused.

Sandy thought she had seldom seen anyone quite as spectacular as Lisa Carnaby. She was very tall, fine boned and slender. Her makeup was immaculate, and her silvery blond hair fitted around her skull like a helmet, not one hair out of place. Everything about her had that same seamless perfection. Her tailored suit was a revelation to Sandy, for all her study of clothes. It was loose enough to drape beautifully, but the black silk jersey underneath fit like a second skin. Sandy was impressed.

Lisa meanwhile was studying Sandy with equal interest. "Put the folder on my desk," she suggested. "Sit down for a moment. Relax. Tell me about yourself."

It sounded friendly enough, but Sandy felt uneasy. Her job had nothing to do with Lisa's. There was no real reason why Lisa should take an interest in her, and she had an odd feeling that Lisa, in spite of that charming smile, had no liking for her.

"Oh, for heaven's sake, sit," Lisa said in a

crisper, less kindly tone. "I understand Jason Grant introduced you to Moffat. Where did he pick you up?"

Sandy's hackles began to rise. She was not easily offended, but there was something about this woman's tone as well as her unfortunate choice of words that riled her.

"He asked my advice about fabrics for his play." Sandy started edging toward the door.

"Another play?" Lisa demanded. "Is he still wasting time on plays? I thought we'd seen the end of that nonsense. Are you involved in this too?"

"Costumes," Sandy murmured vaguely, "that sort of thing."

Lisa tapped one perfect index finger against her desk. "Come back for a moment. You must tell me—"

But Sandy was safely through the door. "I have to be getting back," she mumbled and made her escape.

One thing was plain to her. Lisa did not like Jason Grant, and she certainly liked Sandra Childs even less.

"It's the theater project she doesn't like," Mrs. Moffat explained. "She thinks it's a waste of time, and, who knows, maybe she's right."

"But Jason has permission to do it, doesn't he? You bulldozed that through for him."

"Me?" Mrs. Moffat looked utterly surprised,

then laughed. "Sandy, child, whatever gave you the idea that Jason Grant needs me to run interference for him?"

"Well, you do, don't you?" Sandy was embarrassed. "I mean, you got him his job, didn't you? You're an old friend. He told me so. And he obviously hasn't been able to make a living as an actor. I mean—he's pretty broke, isn't he?"

"He is?"

"Those beat-up old clothes he wears. . . . Why, he doesn't even have a decent winter coat."

Mrs. Moffat shook her head in wonder. "Jason didn't tell you what he's doing here?"

"I haven't seen him since that first day," Sandy admitted doubtfully, "so I don't really know what sort of job he's got. I rather thought he must be working in shipping or in the stockroom, something that doesn't pay much. That's why I thought you must have gotten permission for him to use the auditorium."

"Oh, Sandy," Mrs. Moffat said, shaking her head, "you've made up a fairy tale for yourself. Our friend Jason Grant doesn't just work at Brae-Mill. He *is* Brae-Mill, barring a few stockholders, not one of whom holds as many shares as he and his grandfather own between them."

Sandy felt herself blushing furiously. "I've made a fool of myself, haven't I?"

"It's not your fault. Jason should have told you, but he probably forgot. He likes to pretend that he has no responsibilities around here at all."

Sandy found herself rushing to Jason's defense. "He's a theater person. I overheard someone saying that he was a very good director, and I'm sure he's a good actor too."

"Maybe he is," Mrs. Moffat said gently. "I know nothing about that side of it, only that Mr. Miller hit the ceiling when he found out that Jason had switched his major to theater during his sophomore year in college."

"Mr. Jerome Miller? You mean he's Jason's grandfather?"

"The great man himself." Mrs. Moffat smiled grimly. "Jason's grandpa, and a terrible man when he's crossed. At first I thought he'd send for a hit man. He was in such a rage. The next day he called in his attorneys and formally disowned Jason. A week later, he wrote to the college, threatening to sue them, but by then Jason had left the school and was working in summer stock."

"I know," Sandy murmured softly. "He was very good."

"I don't think Mr. Miller appreciated that," Mrs. Moffat said drily. "He hired a private detective to find the boy and bring him back, by force if necessary. When that didn't work, he decided to have a heart attack, and that did bring Jason to heel."

"But he wants to act and direct plays," Sandy protested. "It's not fair."

"He also wants his grandfather to be happy, because he loves the old man. I can't imagine why."

"Is he awful?"

"You bet." Mrs. Moffat's hands were clenched. "Jerome Miller belongs to the old breed of factory owners, the ones our union broke their hearts over. His motto is 'Take what you want. If you can't buy out the opposition, break it.' "

"And Jason was forced to sell out," Sandy said sadly.

"Not quite." Mrs. Moffat's hands relaxed and became gentle again. "There's too much of the old man in him to ever give up. They made a deal. Jason learns the business, and in return he can have a theater to play with."

The more Sandy thought about her mistake, the more foolish she felt. She began to hope that Jason Grant would stay away from her, so that she wouldn't have to face him again.

And yet, when he stuck his head into the door on Friday, just as she was getting ready to leave, her heart soared with joy.

"How's the job treating you?" he asked. "Has Mrs. Moffat broken your back yet, the wicked old slave driver?"

"Thank you, Mr. Grant," Sandy said primly, "I think I'm going to work out."

"Mr. Grant?" he said, raising one eyebrow. "Since when so formal? It's Jason, remember? I was Jason when you saved me from the dragon lady and I lured you away to this den of iniquity. Are you still bearing malice because I so rudely chucked you into a cab, with you, poor girl, pitifully hollering for help?"

"You should have let me wait for the bus," Sandy said, avoiding his eyes. "It's an excellent connection."

"Our connection, however, seems to have broken down. Hey, Sandy, remember me? I'm the man who got you this rotten, underpaid job. You owe me a debt of gratitude—or at least your company at dinner. Have you eaten anything lately?"

His ridiculous way of jumping from one subject to the next had its customary effect on Sandy. She found herself smiling.

"Now we're back to normal," Jason announced, looking pleased. "I see Mrs. Moffat's left you to lock up. Turn off the lights and let's get out of here."

Sandy found herself following his instructions. She felt befuddled. Jason still looked like a hobo, but now that she knew who he was, she could see that all his worn clothing was of excellent quality. These rags had probably cost more than Pete spent on his natty wardrobe in a whole year.

"I've got to get home," she protested without much conviction.

"Didn't I get you home the last time?" he demanded. "Not in the best approved tradition, I admit. I should have jumped into the cab with you. I would have tried to kiss you. You would have resisted. We could have grappled all the way, and finally you would have slapped my face. I think that's why I didn't do it. I hate being slapped. I once had to play a part that involved being slapped by the heroine. She was quite deft about it, managed to create a marvelous slapping sound without actually connecting with my cheek, but I hated it. It's not the pain, you see. It's the humiliation."

"I wouldn't have slapped you," Sandy protested. Then she realized how that sounded, and she blushed furiously.

Jason laughed. "Now she tells me. But I don't believe you. You are not the sort of girl who snuggles up to a relative stranger in the back of a car."

"What sort of girl do you think I am?"

"A nice girl," he said promptly. "A nice, friendly girl, who allows a guy to kiss her the third time out. We've had one dinner and a lunch, but that was just a small hamburger and the French fries were cold, so it probably doesn't count. If I want to improve my standing, I'll have to persuade you to let me buy you a dinner. I think Joe still owes me some money. You know, the change I didn't pick up last time. Let's see what he's got simmering on the back burner."

Jason was irresistible. Sandy allowed herself to be drawn along, his arm firm and warm around her waist. The building was almost empty, and the few people they met on the way out paid no attention to them. It was Friday, after all, and everyone was eager to get home.

Joe was noisily delighted to see them.

"This time you come in time," he crowed. "Now you shall have a proper Greek dinner. And don't go sitting down at the counter. That's okay for snacks. For real food you sit in the booth."

Sandy remembered the so-called snack he had served them before and wondered what would constitute a real meal.

"I'm not very hungry," she whispered into Jason's ear. "Please don't let him get a big meal for me."

"Not hungry?" Jason demanded, looking shocked and indignant. "You dare to come in here without a good appetite? You ought to be ashamed of yourself. Joe is Greek. He is also a superb cook and has the temperament of a Jewish mother. If you don't eat his food, you reject him personally. Are you really willing to break a good man's heart?"

"I had lunch at the cafeteria," Sandy protested, "the blue-plate special, at least two thousand calories, and they're still there, right under my rib cage."

Jason looked grave. "I know all about that blue-plate special. It is a dastardly trap and should be forbidden by law."

"If only you'd given me fair warning," Sandy mourned. "I could have planned ahead, gone into training. With a week of strict dieting behind me, I could probably have worked my way through Joe's meal and asked for seconds."

"Too late," Jason said sternly. "It's always too late for the noblest of plans. Have you noticed that too? But we can't avoid Joe's dinner. You'll just have to fake it."

"How does one fake eating a meal?" Sandy could imagine an actor faking joy or sorrow, but eating?

"Nothing to it," Jason assured her. "You begin by looking very hungry and enormously enthusiastic when Joe brings the food. Then you attack the plate, and tear everything on it to shreds."

"Then you still have a plateful of messed-up food," Sandy protested, trying not to laugh.

"Aha," Jason said smugly. "That's where real art comes in. You have to be deft about it. Raise a loaded fork toward your mouth, and drop the food on the way. That part's easy. If the fork is ridiculously overloaded, all it takes is a tiny tilting motion. Now comes the tricky bit. You insert empty fork in mouth and roll your eyes in ecstasy, withdraw fork, chew vigorously, swallow, wipe your lips with your napkin, and take a sip of water."

"I think I can manage all that," Sandy admitted. "But when all's said and done, you still have that plate of food in front of you."

"That is true." Jason frowned and considered the problem. "There are several techniques for dealing with that. The method of choice is having a dog. He sits at your feet and catches any bit of food that happens to fall before it ever touches the floor. A dog like that is worth his weight in gold."

"I can see that," Sandy agreed. "But—"

Jason looked solemn. "We have no dog. It is my fate never to be properly equipped in times of crisis. Someday I shall have to tell you about our production of *Kiss Me, Kate.*"

"Was it good?"

"It was disastrous, and all because of my lack of proper planning. It's my tragic flaw. A careful man would have brought a dog."

"No dog," Sandy agreed. "Not even a little one. It's very sad."

"Cats are quite useless," Jason informed her. "I know you'd like to talk me into trying out cats, and I have known some cats who had the intelligence and the appetite. And yet I don't think they would cooperate. Cats lack team spirit. I think that's what it is."

"You may well be right," Sandy agreed with a straight face. "I'll give up the idea of cats. How about parakeets?"

"Parakeets?" His eyes were wide with wonder. "Of course! Why didn't I think of that myself? Sandy, you're a wonderful woman. And here comes Joe, and not a moment too soon. Joe, what took you so long? This poor girl's almost faint with hunger."

Sandy was almost faint with laughter by the time they had worked their way through Joe's prodigious meal. They played the pretend-to-eat game, and when Joe came to take away their still-full plates, they assured him cheerfully that it was the best food they had ever eaten. He seemed satisfied.

"This time I go home by bus," Sandy said. "I'm not being dumped into a cab a second time."

"Cab?" Jason demanded. "Who said anything about a cab? I'm taking you home in style. Will a limousine be all right?"

"I keep forgetting that you're rich." Suddenly Sandy felt rather forlorn. "You see, that's why I got so upset at the way you were throwing money around. I thought you were terribly poor. And you did say that you didn't have a car."

"I don't," he admitted. "I had a license once, but I let it lapse, and then it just seemed more trouble than it was worth. The limo belongs to Grandpa, who never drives, either. He thinks it's a waste of time. Why should he concentrate on the road when he can be leaning back against the upholstery, thinking up lovely new ways of cutting the throats of the competition?"

For Sandy some of the magic had gone out of the evening. "I sort of forgot who you were," she said soberly. "We were having fun."

"And hardworking businessmen aren't supposed to have fun? How about part-time directors? Surely they deserve some beer and skittles."

"What are skittles? And why beer? And why do you have to make a joke out of everything?"

He regarded her quizzically. "No good, eh? All right, Miss Childs, we will be serious. I shall walk you to Public Square and ride the bus home with you. That's how serious I am."

"But I don't want you to—"

"You are the worst woman I ever met for insisting on getting her own way. Just this once, Sandy, give over and let me make a decision."

She felt helpless in the face of his absurdity and made no further protest when he boarded the bus behind her.

"Oops," he said, searching through his pockets. "I don't seem to have any cash on me. Will you pay?"

She dropped two tokens into the fare box, and they sat in the back of the bus, holding hands and smiling at each other.

"I don't know when I've had such a good

time," Jason said when they arrived at her door. "Thank you, Sandy."

He leaned down and kissed her lightly on the cheek, then turned and started walking away.

"Stop!" Sandy cried, running after him. "Jason, come back!"

He turned, surprised and delighted. "Miss Childs, this is undignified, improper, and not in keeping with your high standards of behavior. Surely your mother told you that you must not chase men down the street in full moonlight."

"But you have no money for the bus," Sandy gasped, fighting for breath. "Remember?" She pushed a bus token into his hand.

Jason examined the token carefully, as though it were something very rare and precious, then slipped it into his pocket.

"That was nice," he said softly. "You really cared enough to chase after me, rather than let me walk home. I don't think anyone has ever taken that much thought for my welfare. I'm afraid I will have to kiss you properly for that."

And he did.

Chapter Seven

*S*andy waited for a phone call from Jason. She spent the weekend at home, piling her library books on the couch close to the phone, trying to persuade herself that she really was studying and not waiting for his call. She despised herself for wasting so much time and tried hard to concentrate on the books, which were interesting and informative.

But even while she was submerged in the books, her fingers busily taking notes and making sketches, her traitorous ears were tuned in to that first hiccup the phone always gave before it started to ring seriously. From time to time, she found herself sitting quite still, her eyes tightly closed, willing the phone to ring. She tried to conjure up the sound, as if she could force the phone to ring by sheer willpower.

She stayed up late Saturday night, slept badly, and got up early to renew her vigil.

On Sunday afternoon the phone finally rang.

Notebook, sketch pad, and books went flying as Sandy lunged for the receiver. It was her mother.

"Hi, Mom," she said, ashamed at the sinking feeling in her stomach. "Is everything okay?"

"I hope so, Sandy. You tell me. Is it?" Sandy could almost see her mother, the gray-streaked blond hair falling forward over her eyes, the faint smile, the way she sat, one leg folded under her like a teenager. "It's weird having to ask you how you are, not knowing. I wish you weren't so far away. Bill came in from Toledo, and Tod is here too. We all miss you."

Sandy was ashamed because she hadn't even been thinking about them. "Next time you expect a family reunion, let me know in advance, and I'll be there."

"I wasn't expecting them," Martha Childs admitted. "I mean, I was expecting Tod, but Bill's visit came as a surprise."

"How's he doing?"

"He's been promised a promotion at the end of the year."

"That's great."

"And he's getting married."

"Wow! I thought he and Pat broke up."

"Not Pat, thank goodness. I tried so hard to like that girl, and I never could. He met a girl in Toledo. He's bringing her here in four weeks' time. I think we'll have time to paint Tod's old room. The walls got ruined when we took down those Spiderman posters. Off-white, do you think, or pink?"

"How about a rosy sort of off-white?"

"Lovely idea. Her name's Elizabeth, but her parents call her Betsy, and Bill calls her Shorty. What do you think we should call her?"

Sandy giggled. Her mother occasionally ran into problems with names. Once she had failed to catch a man's name during the introduction but had overheard his wife calling him Pops. Years later, she was still being teased about addressing a perfect stranger as Pops.

"You'd better call her Betsy," Sandy suggested. "Is she nice?"

"She sounds darling." Martha sounded enthusiastic. "She runs a health-food store and teaches exercise classes. And she really is short, tiny. She barely comes up to Bill's shoulder in the snapshot he showed us, and she has such a sweet face. I wish you could come and meet her."

Sandy did some hasty arithmetic in her head. "I'll be there," she promised. "If I hop on the bus straight from work on Friday. . . ."

"Oh, dear." Martha suddenly sounded woeful. "That bus doesn't run anymore. Didn't you know? I wish you had a car. Dad was saying just the other day that perhaps now, with a new job, you could afford to buy one. He's even got Dave looking for a nice trade-in for you. Aren't you glad you have a brother working for a dealership?"

"It'll be some time before I can afford a car. I'm earning less here than at the shop. Now, Mom, don't get upset. I'm getting a lot of valuable training for free. It's a good deal—really."

"But how are you going to get here?" Martha sounded as disappointed as a child. "It would be so nice if we could all be together to welcome Shor—I mean Betsy. Tod will be here again, and Dave's bringing his latest girl. That boy's never going to settle down. I can just see him as a lonely old bachelor. Maybe seeing Bill so happy might give him ideas."

"Dave has ideas," Sandy said with a private grin. "Lots of ideas. The trouble is, they're not marrying ideas."

Martha refused to laugh. "That can get very dull, dear, and lonely. A man needs something stable in life, something to build on."

"A game plan," Sandy suggested, thinking about Meg and her problem.

"I suppose you can call it that." Martha sounded doubtful. "When I was growing up, we went overboard on the planning bit. It was okay to work, but marriage was definitely your first priority. If you weren't engaged by the time you were twenty-one, you got very worried."

"But a lot of girls went to college," Sandy said wistfully.

"You sound jealous," Martha said with a sigh. "It was easier then to get into college, more affordable. A lot of my friends went, but the only degree they seemed to be working for was the MRS. They didn't really want an education."

"What a waste." Sandy thought about all those expensive courses at the Art Institute.

Martha was wryly amused. "I don't think they felt the time was wasted. An education did make it easier to find work before the children came along. And I think a lot of women saw a career as something to fall back on—in case they were one of the unfortunate few who couldn't find a husband."

"You're making it up. It wasn't really like that, was it?"

"It was pretty awful. We started worrying about catching a man even before we went to college, and of course high-school boys weren't all that interesting. But I was engaged by the time I was twenty-one, and I had a ring to prove it. It was a beautiful ring in the shape of a daisy. I just hated to give it back, but Harve was the wrong man."

"Why did you get engaged to him, then?"

"The time seemed right—and he had a nice car, a red Pontiac, custom paint job, gorgeous."

"Oh, Mom," Sandy protested, "you fell in love with a car."

"It was a very special car, dear, and the ring was out of sight."

"Would you have stayed married to him," Sandy demanded curiously, "if you had gone through with it?"

There was a thoughtful silence at the other end of the wire.

"I don't know," Martha finally admitted. "Lots of those early marriages didn't work out. Two of my friends got a divorce—four divorces in fact. At least Debbie's second marriage has worked out, but Karen Ford has racked up three bad marriages."

"I remember Mrs. Ford. She used to be so pretty."

"Still is, and still looking for Mr. Right."

"I'll keep my fingers crossed for her. But, Mom, we've got to stop gabbing. This must be costing you an arm and a leg."

"Sunday rates, Sandy. But you're right. Once I get started, I just hate to hang up. I miss you so. We all do. And we worry. That's really why I called. Bill heard from his friend, that nice Peter Brooks, that you're not going out with him anymore. We sort of hoped. . . . And he could have driven you home. Your Aunt Kate doesn't mind putting up our overflow, and she has two guest rooms. So, how are you going to find a ride? I don't suppose you would consider calling Peter and asking him?"

"No," Sandy said firmly. "I can't do that, but I will try to come. Maybe Meg can be persuaded, or someone. . . . I'll work on it."

"Perhaps Tod can come and fetch you, although it would take him a bit out of his way."

"Three hundred eighty miles out of his way.

No, Mom, don't even suggest it. I'll think of a way."

"In four weeks?" Meg wailed. "But, Sandy, that's the big open house on Derbyshire. Come to think of it, all my weekends are shot. That's what you get in the realty business. It's the only time working couples can go house hunting. Can't you rent a car?"

"Money," Sandy explained. "That lovely stuff, which I don't have."

"I could lend you a few bucks."

"You're a pal. But I wouldn't be able to pay it back for months, if ever. You're already paying for my groceries. I can't accept any more."

"Something will turn up," Meg promised, optimistic as ever. "It always does."

In spite of the nice call from her mother, Sandy decided that the weekend had been a failure. She had to renew the books for another two weeks, not really having understood what she was reading. She knew it was the result of poor concentration, and she was annoyed with herself. Why, in heaven's name, should Jason call her? *But,* insisted another part of her mind, *why didn't he want to?* He had kissed her as if he really meant it. He had looked at her in a way that made her feel. . . . She couldn't put her finger on it. How did he make her feel? Important, or at least important to him. That was it. So why hadn't he called?

Mrs. Moffat had not had a good weekend, either.

"Every year I promise myself to get flu shots," she mourned. "And every year I forget. This isn't even a full-blown flu. It's just enough to make me miserable. My throat feels like sandpaper."

"Hot tea," Sandy suggested. "Tea with lemon and honey. That helps."

Mrs. Moffat coughed. "Tea does sound good. Run down to the cafeteria and ask them to make some for me. Have Claire put it in one of those thermos jugs. We'll get it back to her before the end of the day."

Sandy ran down the stairs. Waiting for the elevator was always a drag, and she dressed for comfort these days—jeans, sweatshirt, and running shoes.

The cafeteria was a large, brightly lit room filled with plastic-covered tables. There was the usual smell of soap and hot grease, pleasant enough when you were hungry, but not first thing in the morning.

Claire said, "Tea?" Sandy might have been asking for something strange and exotic. "Never before eleven. It takes time to get the urns heated up. Don't you have one of those little electric pots for boiling water? I thought all the offices had them."

Sandy explained that they weren't exactly an office, and no, they did not have a hot pot. Could they borrow one?

Claire was eager to help. The sales department was sure to have extra hot pots, she said; they ordered them by the dozen.

"I'll put the tea bags inside the thermos for you, and the honey and lemon juice in this screw-top jar. You'll need a long spoon. There you are. I hope Mrs. Moffat feels better soon."

Sandy raced back up to the first floor and found a conference in session in the hallway. There were several people she had already met, including Lisa Carnaby, dazzling as usual, in gray flannel today with a cream-colored silk shirt.

"My goodness!" Lisa exclaimed. "It's the child from the cutting-room floor. Have you lost your way?"

Sandy flushed. "I'm trying to borrow a hot pot for Mrs. Moffat."

Lisa was amused. "A hot pot? Won't a luke-warm pot do?"

Sandy wished with all her heart that Lisa would simply step aside and let her get on with her errand. "A small electric device for heating water," she snapped. "They told me in the cafeteria that several of them are in use on this floor."

"You mean the contraptions the secretaries use to brew their ghastly diet messes." Lisa had obviously never needed to go on a diet. She made the whole idea sound ridiculous.

"Why don't we let the young lady get on with her job," an older man suggested. "We can move our discussion into my office. If you would bring along your charts, Lisa, we should be able to put together something to show Jason tomorrow morning."

"We'll have to do better than that," Sandy heard Lisa saying as the group started to move toward an open door. "Jason's back in town. He'll be coming in after lunch."

It gave Sandy a nasty little shock to hear Lisa pronounce Jason's name. She said it as if she knew him so well, but then, they had probably been working together for a long time.

She borrowed the hot pot and made tea for Mrs. Moffat.

"It does help," the older woman rasped, "but I'd better go home after all. I think I'm running a fever. There's no need to pass the bug around."

Sandy agreed that bed was probably the best place.

"I would never have come in, except for Jason. His actors are coming in tonight, and he'll want to see what we have done about costumes."

"But we haven't—"

Mrs. Moffat nodded sadly. "I thought we would work on it today and have something to show him, at least some ideas."

"I can work on it," Sandy suggested eagerly.

"I've read the play, and I've been thinking about it."

Mrs. Moffat looked relieved. "You don't mind staying late?"

"Not a bit." Sandy's heart was hammering.

Mrs. Moffat sighed. "It won't be a proper rehearsal, just a walk-through. They read from the script and find out where they're supposed to stand. It's not very interesting." She wrapped a scarf around throat and chin, then pulled her knitted cap down almost to her nose. "I hate being sick. It's a waste of time, and there's so much to do. I'll come in tomorrow, if possible. Next fall I'm getting those flu shots—if only I don't forget again."

Sandy spent the day preparing for *The Cinderella Game.* She made sketches for several sets— an antechamber in the Senate Building, and Cindy's office. That one wasn't really a set, just a backdrop painted with rows of files and bookcases, with portraits of politicians staring down from the wall. It had a nice, dusty, claustrophobic look to it. A girl would simply hate being relegated to such a stuffy cubbyhole while the interesting, exciting part of the job took place somewhere else.

For the ballroom scene, Sandy had created several sketches. She had already spent days poring over photos of White House interiors and had finally come up with four different versions of the same basic idea. The action took place in a foyer leading to the ballroom. Sandy had drawn a central arch with a reception area behind it. Descending from that were two shallow steps, with a columned entrance to the ballroom itself on the left, angled so that the audience could not actually look into it. On the right was a door leading to a cloakroom.

Sandy sketched Cynthia Madison, the Cinderella girl, poised in the archway. Cynthia, called Cindy, of course, was wearing the red ball gown, her hands raised to shed the diaphanous cloak that floated out behind her. Pleased with the effect, Sandy added Senator John Prince standing in the ballroom entrance, handsome and manly in black, his white shirtfront gleaming. She wondered if senators ever wore decorations. A brilliant slash of red ribbon across the chest would have added a nice bit of color.

It would be easier, she thought, once she knew what the prince—that is, the senator—looked like. Surely he would have to be tall, slim, and very handsome. It seemed a pity that Jason wasn't playing the part himself.

There was only one ugly sister in this play, but that one was more than enough, almost too horrid to be believable, a real witch. Sandy couldn't imagine her at all. Being a congresswoman with a seat on an important committee, she had to be clever, of course, and attractive. How could a clever, good-looking woman be made to appear so repulsive? Sandy had tentatively dressed her in a mannish-looking suit with monstrously padded shoulders for the earlier scene, but the ball gown had her stymied.

She finally decided that Cat Raucus—what a name!—would wear a slinky gown slit almost to the hip, in a poisonous shade of green.

Jason surprised her by coming in so quietly that she was not aware of him until he was right behind her chair, his arms around her.

"You've been working on my play," he murmured, resting his cheek against hers. "What a nice girl you are."

"Nice woman," she countered. *"Girl* is a fighting word. Ask Mrs. Moffat."

"You are an exceptionally nice woman, and I like your work." He picked up the next sheet. "If that dress is meant for Cat, we'll have to put her on a diet. Polly's quite happy playing ugly. She'll gladly play ridiculous, but she won't try to squeeze into anything like that. Show me the rest of your drawings."

He sat down beside her, and they pored over the sketches together. He looked different today, Sandy decided. It was partly the suit, the three-piece suit that was almost a uniform, complete with the obligatory dark-red tie and an edge of the matching handkerchief protruding just the right amount. He had also had his hair cut, an artful cut that showed off the nice shape of his skull. Nobody would have taken him for a down-and-out actor today.

"I like what you've done with the office," he was saying, quite unaware of her scrutiny. "But we need a desk and two chairs. The desk is referred to, but not used, so you could make it part of the backdrop—right here. You could use a forced perspective. Then the chairs would go here and here." He lightly penciled in his additions.

Sandy nodded eagerly.

"The ballroom set will have to be deeper than that, but the basic idea is good. A good part of the action takes place behind your arch. So if we widen it—like this—and raise that part of the stage. . . . The trouble with that is that we'd lose all that lovely detail you've lavished on the archway. It looks very authentic."

"White House 1955," Sandy admitted. "We can use those details on the back wall instead. Look." Her pencil flew over a clean sheet of paper. "We can bring the arch to the very edge of the ballroom entrance, so that now the reception area is defined only by these two steps."

"Make it four steps," Jason suggested. "That gives us a nice sweep, not quite as shallow, otherwise we end up tripping off the edge of the stage—where the footlights ought to be."

"Do you need footlights?"

"Not really," he said. "Not when I have such good designs to work with."

Sandy thought how happy he looked when he

talked about the play, and she hated his grandfather for taking him away from it.

Jason was leaning back in the chair, his arms locked behind his head, his eyes dreamy. "We'll fill in with floods from the sides and back. Footlights went the way of all things about the time they stopped putting in prompt boxes. Which reminds me, we're going to need a prompter. Except for Polly and Gus, we have no one with experience."

"But Cynthia Madison, I mean Deb—"

"Deb's never had to speak more than three lines in any one scene. Normally she whispers a couple of words, then bursts into song. The orchestra comes up behind her, and she starts swirling. She does swirl very competently, but I have my hopes pinned on Polly and Gus. You haven't met them yet, have you? Let's go and turn on the lights. Our cast will be assembling soon."

Chapter Eight

*T*he auditorium was different tonight. The modeling ramp and the pleated screen were gone. Jason turned up the lights on the stage and arranged nine chairs in a circle.

"It's tight," he complained, "a foretaste of what our problem is going to be. There will be nine of us crammed into this space. Gus is bringing someone to do lights and props. Last time we used a girl from advertising who had a nice eye for detail, but no sense of timing whatsoever. Did you bring your script?"

Sandy laid the sketches under one of the chairs and waved her copy of the play.

"Good. You'll have to take notes for me. Do you know shorthand?"

Sandy sadly shook her head.

"Not important," Jason assured her. "Just keep this pad on your lap and write down what I say."

Sandy turned pale. "Do I have to be able to read it back to you?"

109

"Not to worry, just things like 'enter left,' 'turn upstage,' 'pick up ashtray'—that sort of thing. Figure out your own notation system, so we can combine it with the script later on."

"But—"

"You'll get the idea as we go along." He jumped up and peered over her head to the back of the auditorium. "Here they are, only ten minutes late. Wonders will never cease."

The three professional actors swept in, with four Brae-Mill employees straggling behind them. Sandy was pleased to see Tracy from the cutting room, looking quite pretty without the disguising coveralls. She looked nervous and excited but managed a quick smile in Sandy's direction. The amateurs sat silent and respectful, while the professionals immediately began to talk across each other. Sandy thought she had never met people so enthralled by the sound of their own voices.

Deb had changed her hairstyle. It was just as spiky tonight, but the sides were even shorter, almost shaved, and had been dyed purple. A wig would be essential, Sandy decided. A punk Cinderella just did not fit the bill. Jason, however, did not appear perturbed by his leading lady's odd appearance. Perhaps in his mind's eye he already saw her wigged and costumed for the part of Cindy.

Polly turned out to be the plump, middle-aged woman from the Italian restaurant, the one who had worked so hard to persuade Deb to try out for the part. Tonight her gray hair hung in a thick braid down the middle of her back, and she wore a tentlike caftan.

"It has pockets," she explained, and, to prove the point, she extracted her script, a pad and pencil, cigarettes, a lighter, a compact, a lipstick, and a package of throat lozenges and arranged them in her lap. Her rich, melodious voice made everything she said sound important. "Why all these chairs, Jason? Aren't we going to have a walk-through tonight?"

"Not yet," Jason explained. "We have a few newcomers who might prefer to simply read the play all the way through this first time." He introduced the four amateurs, who smiled nervously, clutching their scripts. Sandy recognized Susan, the middle-aged woman from the payroll office, and the long-haired boy from shipping. She couldn't place the other man, but thought he would have made a more convincing prince than Gus, who was bald, paunchy, and not young enough.

"Gloria couldn't make it tonight," Gus announced in a thin, querulous voice, "after promising faithfully and all."

"That's too bad," Jason said without sounding too perturbed. "Will we have to find someone else?"

"Oh, she'll be here by and by. Gloria's got her

eye on the big time and she badly wants to get into production."

"You mean she has no experience?" Now Jason did sound upset.

"Assistant to an assistant, poor girl, but she's a pusher."

Jason frowned. "What did you promise her? Does she know that this is not a professional production?"

Gus shrugged. "She knows, but she really is interested in doing the lights and doesn't much mind doing props. What she's after is the credit as stage manager."

"If that's all." Jason laughed. "If she does a good job, I'll see that she gets a glowing write-up in the Sunday paper. Shall we get started?"

Magically all the chatter dried up. Deb, who had been telling the world about a problem with her agent, stopped abruptly and became attentive. Polly stubbed out her cigarette and dropped part of her belongings back into her pockets. Gus put on horn-rimmed glasses, which made him look less than ever like a Prince Charming, and Tracy crossed her legs and moistened her lips.

"Act one, scene one," Jason said. "Cindy and John—you're on."

The reading was a mess. The pros read fast, enunciating clearly and without emotion, while the amateurs tried desperately to infuse their lines with suitable expression. They stopped, stumbled, and frequently lost their place. Jason remained amiable throughout, even when Susan got a coughing fit and Tracy developed a nervous giggle that almost put her out of commission.

"It's the first reading," he said kindly. "Once you're sure of your lines and get a feel for the play, you'll forget all about yourself and become the character. I really appreciate your giving up so much time for this. I hope it'll be fun for you. I'm certainly looking forward to it. See you on Wednesday."

The Brae-Mill contingent left, smiling and nodding. Sandy wondered whether this was her cue to exit, and began to pack up her belongings.

"Don't go running off," Jason protested. "We need you. Were you able to keep track?"

Sandy looked through her notes. "Sort of. In the second scene, you want a diversion of some sort, either people walking through or a small group in the back—"

"Upstage," Polly corrected her. "There is a back to a stage, but the audience can't see it."

"A small group upstage having a quiet conversation." Sandy didn't see what difference it made, but Polly looked satisfied.

"And then in Act Three, line twenty-five, you said you wanted a fade up." She rattled off the rest of the notes she had made, not sure whether any of them made sense.

Jason seemed pleased. "Sandy's designing

scenery and costumes," he explained to the others. "She's brought her preliminary drawings."

Sandy had not been sure until now that he was actually planning to use her designs. She blushed with pleasure and fished her drawings out from under the chair. They were passed around and discussed.

"Not much room," Deb protested, looking at the ballroom set.

"That's the one we're going to change," Sandy explained eagerly. "We're moving the arch forward and opening it up, and there will be four steps for you."

Deb nodded, satisfied. "Is that going to be the dress? Red? Cinderella's always in white, isn't she?"

"Exactly!" Jason sounded triumphant. "But our Cinderella is not your standard bland fairy princess. Cindy Madison is an intelligent, passionate woman." He threw a quick grin at Sandy. "Not a girl. And remember, Deb, we won't have a sea of swirling dresses to set you against. Cindy has to make a statement by herself. She has to rivet the eye."

Deb was pacified, and the discussion moved on to Polly's ball gown. She examined Sandy's slinky design and laughed heartily.

"Oh, honey," she said, "not even twenty years ago. I mean, can you imagine me?"

Sandy nodded. "Jason told me this wouldn't work, but I've had another idea." She turned to a clean page and started sketching. A squat, powerful figure appeared under her fingers. The shoulders were padded and extended even further with epaulettes. A heavy scarf was attached to the center of the back and draped to the floor, coming to a point. There were points on the long, tight sleeves, coming down over the hands, almost to the fingertips. "Green," she explained. "Lizard green, with flecks of black."

Polly was enchanted. "In a dress like that, I can make Cat reptilian. I wasn't sure how I could play her nasty enough, but this is it. My goodness, but you do know your job."

"But I only just—" Sandy began, pleased and embarrassed.

Jason cut her off. "Sandy does pattern making and has a special interest in theater design."

Gus stood up and shrugged peevishly. "I hope we're through for tonight. I don't know about the rest of you, but I have an early call tomorrow morning, a voice-over for Harris Advertising."

Then he turned to Sandy, took off his glasses, and really looked at her. Sandy realized with a start that he could look quite attractive. He took both her hands, holding them as if they were about to dance. His eyes became warm and intent.

"This has been a great pleasure," he said in a completely different voice.

Sandy was caught off balance. Gus no longer looked bad tempered. His voice was a good two octaves lower than before, and he sounded deeply sincere. For the first time she could see him as the hero.

"I was wondering if you couldn't wear a decoration with your evening dress in the third act," she blurted out. "A medal on a red ribbon perhaps. That would tie you in with Cindy."

"That's a marvelous idea." He patted her hand and became middle-aged again. "You are a nice child. Good night, all."

When the actors had left, Sandy helped Jason fold up the chairs and stack them against the walls.

"Now, on to Joe's. You can drop off the sketch pad, but you'll need to bring the notebook and the script. We'll do some work over dinner."

He held Sandy's coat for her and picked up his disreputable wool scarf.

"I somehow thought you would be wearing a coat," she said.

"Since I'm in uniform today? There's a limit to how far I'm willing to conform. The executive uniform for the board, okay. But I'm not giving up my Doctor Who scarf for anyone. It's lucky, it's warm, and it doesn't restrict movement. As a matter of fact, it is the ultimate garment, except for one minor flaw—the fringe seems to pick up a lot of dirt. Someday you will design a self-cleaning scarf for me."

"They liked my drawings," Sandy boasted, still dazzled by her success.

"Of course!" Jason was matter-of-fact. "You're good. Didn't you know that? Why do you think I got you involved in this?"

Sandy had rather hoped that he had brought her along because he liked her. She was glad he liked her work, of course, but was left feeling uncertain again. Jason talked to her as if he liked her a lot. He looked at her as if she was special to him. He had kissed her—not casually. But then again, theater people seemed to go in for extravagant gestures. Look at the way Gus had behaved. And Jason hadn't called her since that memorable kiss. But then again, according to Lisa he had been out of town.

So she followed him down the alley to Joe's diner and allowed him to order gyros and coffee for both of them.

There were no games tonight, no nonsense at all. Jason's mind was solidly on the play.

"What do you think of the cast?" he began right away.

Sandy felt helpless. She had no valuable opinions to offer. Gus had seemed wrong to her, and now she realized that he could be fascinating when he wanted to be. "Polly has a good voice," she said hesitantly, "doesn't she?"

"Yes, yes," Jason agreed impatiently. It was after all not her opinion he was after. He needed to express his own. "Gus and Polly are competent, and I feel pretty good about Susan. She's done a lot of little-theater work. She's going to be fine once she gets into the part. George is a natural, and Gary looks so good that he doesn't have to do anything but stand around and dress up the set."

Sandy tried again. "Tracy is very good-looking too."

Jason frowned. "That's no advantage to us. We don't want her to look better than Deb. We may actually have to tone down her looks. I wasn't sure about using her at all, but she's such a nice kid, and she really wants to get a foothold in acting. I think she's serious about it."

"Lots of models go on to become actresses," Sandy suggested doubtfully. "Don't they?"

"Lots of actresses make money on the side modeling," Jason corrected her. "What do you think of our pros?" This time he really seemed to want her opinion.

"Polly is wonderful," Sandy said eagerly. "I'd never have picked her as Cat. She looks so kind and motherly, but she's very good, isn't she?"

"You're so right, and Gus is cut from the same cloth."

"He doesn't look the part."

Jason laughed. "Wait till you see him with his rug on, and a corset to pull in that flabby midsection. Gus can be just as gorgeous as he needs to be. He simply doesn't believe in wasting voice or glamour on a rehearsal. Comes the night, and he'll charm the socks off you."

"He already did," Sandy admitted, "for about thirty seconds."

Jason grinned. "I noticed that he gave you the full treatment. I think he wants something from you, and—come to think of it—he got it: the red ribbon across his manly chest. He'll love that."

"You don't mind?"

"I like it."

"Isn't it ambassadors and generals who wear those things?"

"In the Washington of our making, Sandy, senators are more resplendent than kings—at least charming unmarried senators. No, it's a good idea. Gus can do with a bit of help, even decked out in rug, corset, and his working voice."

"He sounds so different when he's just talking."

"Gus squeaks like a peevish mouse," Jason admitted. "It's a bit off-putting, but it does save the vocal chords for when they're needed. No, Gus is all right. The one I'm not easy about is Deb."

"But you picked her out. I thought—"

Jason leaned across the table, frowning. "It's like this. Cynthia has to look good. She doesn't actually have a lot of lines. Did you notice that? Everyone else talks, mostly Cat and John, while Cindy has very little to say. That's why she has to be a presence. She has to make a statement simply by the way she looks and moves. You are setting her up with her clothes, of course, and

I'll help her all I can with the lighting, but it is a part that demands body language, and Deb has that. It's her dance training."

Sandy was puzzled. "Then she's just about perfect for the part."

"She is," Jason agreed. "She should be. But I have an uneasy feeling in the pit of my stomach that Deb will sail through every rehearsal like a queen and fall flat on her face at showtime." He stared into his cup, looking moody and abstracted.

Sandy finished her coffee, pushed the remains of her gyro to one side of the plate, and stifled a yawn.

"Uh-oh, I've kept you up past your bedtime," Jason said, suddenly aware of her again. "Are you sure you're not going to eat the rest of that food? Then wrap up, and I'll drive you home."

Sandy was grateful for the offer of a ride—and surprised. It had not been a romantic evening this time, and she had not really expected him to take her home.

"Limo or taxi tonight?" she asked.

Jason made a magnificent gesture surely worthy of Senator John Prince and struck a disdainful pose. "Taxi, young woman? A borrowed limo? What do you take me for? Have you somehow gained the impression that I am the sort of man who can't drive his own car?"

Sandy was confused by his sudden switch from

businesslike to frivolous. "You don't have a license."

"Last week I had no license," he admitted with an air of grandeur. "Tonight I do."

"And last week you didn't have a car, either."

"It's like this," Jason said, wrapping his scarf around both of them, so that they ended up nose to nose. "It was the humiliation of having you stake me the bus fare. I said to myself, 'Jason Grant, are you a man or a mouse? Are you the kind of man who allows a woman to support his habit?' "

"What habit?"

"Laziness, a revolting addiction. So I gritted my teeth and said no to passive dependency, taxis, and all that sort of thing. I am now a driving man, and you are the one responsible for my reform. What do you say to that?"

His face was very close to hers, and he was smiling into her eyes. Sandy felt her knees go weak and knew a moment of panic. This man could turn his charm on and off like a light switch. He could ignore her for hours, treat her as a casual coworker, and then turn around and make her feel like this. The danger point Meg had talked about, that moment when you had to draw back, had already come and gone. It was too late.

Chapter Nine

*M*RS. Moffat was sick for the greater part of that week, and Sandy was run off her feet, not so much doing anything as trying to reassure everyone that Mrs. Moffat would come back and catch up on her hundred-and-one obligations.

She was grabbing a sandwich in the cafeteria when Mr. Hicks from the cutting room came and sat down at her table. He was a serious, elderly man, with a prim, schoolmasterly manner.

"The trouble with Mrs. Moffat," he announced, "is that she will not delegate authority. She should have been training a backup team for years. I've never heard of an operation this size that relies on a single pattern maker. We've all tried. I myself sent her five different girls during the last year, and she sent them all back. Not suitable! What does suitable matter? It's just a job and can be learned like any other job. Now, I don't mean to say Mrs. Moffat is conceited. . . ." His tone implied that that was exactly what he wanted to say.

Sandy was getting ready to defend Mrs. Moffat when they were interrupted by a new arrival, one of the secretaries from sales, obviously an old friend of Mr. Hicks's.

"Don't mind me," she said, fussing with her tray. "I'm just so upset, I have to talk to someone. You're Mrs. Moffat's new assistant, aren't you? Sandy Childs? Lisa mentioned you. I wish it were Friday already. This has been such a week."

"Trouble?" Mr. Hicks inquired sympathetically.

The secretary stirred her coffee so vigorously that it slopped all over the table, and she mopped up the mess with shaking fingers. "I'm so sorry. Everything's been like this all day."

"Miss Carnaby on your back again?" Mr. Hicks seemed to have heard the story many times before.

"It's worse this week, because the buyers will start coming in for a look at the summer clothes, and we have nothing new to show them." Both she and Mr. Hicks looked at Sandy sadly and reproachfully.

Sandy realized that someone had to do something. "Perhaps I could run up some of Mrs. Moffat's designs," she suggested hopefully.

The secretary brightened. "Could you? Could you really?"

"Mrs. Moffat started me on the summer portfolio. I'm pretty sure I could do the slack suit

with the halter, the walking shorts, and the sun-
dresses. And I suppose I could try my hand on
the swimsuits too, but—"

"Trying is not enough," Mr. Hicks announced
huffily. "Not when you're working with
spandex."

The secretary laid her hand over Sandy's.
"Please," she said. "See if you can't get out a few
things for Lisa, just something she can trot out
for the buyers, just enough to get her off my
back."

Mr. Hicks was examining Sandy doubtfully.
"So you think you can get out the models by
yourself? I suppose there's no harm in trying."

Sandy gave him a bright smile and hoped she
looked more confident than she felt.

Mr. Hicks had obviously decided that she
looked capable. "I suppose you'll want extra
hands in the sample room." He scowled slightly.
"Well, I was going to send you that girl, Tracy,
anyway." He shrugged irritably. "I've done my
level best with her, but the downtime on that
notcher is getting to be chronic. She has no feeling for the machine. She doesn't listen to it. I'd
fire her, but. . . ."

Sandy grinned. "I know. She's a perfect size
eight."

"That's it precisely, and few people realize
how rare it is." Mr. Hicks examined Sandy
through narrowed eyes. "You have a nice figure,
Miss Childs, but you could never be a model."

"Afraid not," Sandy admitted cheerfully. "I'm a ten from shoulder to hip and a twelve from there on down. That's how I learned to alter patterns, to make them fit."

"Altering patterns is one thing, and making them from scratch is something else," he said glumly. "Don't go out on a limb. Stick with Mrs. Moffat's designs. Just run up a few samples for Miss Carnaby, and pray that she never finds out that you did them on your own."

Tracy arrived, bringing her perfect size-eight body and a glorious sense of confidence. Sandy had trouble believing that this was the same Tracy who had scowled at her broken-down notcher and collapsed in hysterical giggles during the rehearsal.

"Well, it's just a matter of knowing a job," Tracy explained calmly. "I understand clothes, and I've been modeling since junior high. I took a course one summer and started getting jobs on charity shows. Not that I'd ever want to make a career of it. It's all right here, where it's just part of the job. There's none of that cutthroat competition, and I know what I'm talking about. My sister has done modeling in New York, hands and feet mostly, and she told me what it was like. Talk about dog-eat-dog! I don't want to have to fight a dozen other girls for every single job. Anyway, I like the rag trade. I really love clothes."

"So do I," Sandy agreed. "But what got you interested in the play?"

"Oh, that." Tracy seemed uncertain. "Maybe that wasn't such a hot idea. I don't think I have talent, but I thought it might be fun—and maybe useful someday, in case I do get into professional modeling after all. Was I awful?"

"No, you were fine, just a bit nervous, and Jason expected that." Sandy wondered if she should warn Tracy against looking too pretty, but decided not to. Anyway, there was very little the girl could do to tone down what nature had given her—a perfect face and figure. The surprising thing was that she was so nice in spite of it.

"Are you working late?" Tracy asked. "Mr. Hicks seemed to think you'd be working around the clock. I could stay and give you a hand, if you'd help me with my lines. I don't want to make a fool of myself again."

Sandy thought that was a fine idea, and they ended the day going through the script, marking Tracy's lines with yellow highlighter to make it easier for her.

"That does help. Oh, Sandy, I feel so much better about the play now that I know I can come to you for advice."

Sandy protested that she knew absolutely nothing about the theater, but Tracy simply didn't believe her.

"I saw Jason talking to you, and you were taking notes. Maybe you're not an actress, but you're in with the theater crowd."

Sandy explained that her main interest lay in the costumes, and Tracy naturally wanted to see the sketches. She oohed and aahed over the ball gowns, and before Tracy knew it, Sandy had her standing on the platform and was pinning lengths of muslin around her.

"Like that," Sandy was saying triumphantly. "Now turn very slowly. Try not to—"

Tracy never did find out what she was not supposed to do, because that was the moment when Jerome Miller walked into the room.

Sandy had seen the great man from a distance but never so close up, and her first impression was one of energy and rage. He was shorter than Jason, broader and more powerfully built. His large head, with its thick thatch of gray curls, was thrust forward like an angry bull's. He glared intently at the two women, then snapped, "Where is she?"

Tracy gave a little bleat of distress and stood like a statue, immobilized by the folds of muslin and her terror of the boss.

Sandy calmly took the pins out of her mouth, stood up, and said, "Good afternoon, sir. Are you looking for Mrs. Moffat?"

"Fetch her," Mr. Miller snapped, about as conscious of the women as if they were two pieces of furniture.

"I can't," Sandy said reasonably. "She went home."

The blue eyes, surprisingly like Jason's in shape but paler, locked onto Sandy and took inventory of her. "You are her assistant? She's letting you work on the advance models? Is this one of them?"

"Yes, Mr. Miller," Sandy agreed, with a glorious disregard for the truth.

"You're much too young," Mr. Miller snapped contemptuously. "Under thirty, I bet."

"That is correct." Sandy was glad he had not said "under twenty-one." Obviously being tired and overworked added a few useful years to her appearance, and Mrs. Moffat's baggy gray smock helped.

"Wasted years at an art school, I bet," was his next scornful comment.

"No, sir," Sandy said calmly. "My training has all been hands on." There seemed little point in telling him just then that the sum total of her training amounted to less than a month.

"Good," Mr. Miller growled, then, amazingly, he smiled. "What's that you're working on? Is it one of those caftans?"

Sandy tried to see the muslin through his eyes. Could it possibly be fitted into Brae-Mill's output of sports clothes? Luckily it did not yet look like a ball gown. It was merely strips of fabric, with lines of pins running from Tracy's shoulder to the floor. On the other hand, it did not look like any Brae-Mill garment she had ever seen on a rack.

"It's number 6132," she said, blessing the numbering system. Surely the old man would not ask her to describe the model.

For several frightful moments, he simply stared at her, frowning, then nodded. "I haven't seen the 6000 series yet. I didn't even know we had started one. That's Moffat's fault. She doesn't keep me informed. All right, get on with your work."

He left, and Tracy let out a breath that she seemed to have held in all the time Mr. Miller had been in the room. "What is the model you said you were working on? I didn't know we had anything over 5300."

"I made it up," Sandy admitted.

"Then let's hope and pray something distracts him," Tracy said with a pious glance at the ceiling. "Because it would be just like Mr. Miller to follow it up."

Sandy chewed on her lower lip. "Maybe I had better have a real model number ready, and you and I had better be working on it, just in case he comes back."

"But he'll want to know about this one."

Sandy grinned ruefully. "And I'll have to admit that I made a dumb mistake, that it was an experimental model from Mrs. Moffat's private sketchbook, that somehow got mixed up with this year's summer clothes."

Tracy wiggled out of the muslin and got back into her jeans. It was not until she was at the door, fully dressed, that she turned back to Sandy, looking puzzled.

"Why didn't you just tell him that we were working on the play? We're on our own time, aren't we? We have a right to stay late and work for Jason or even for ourselves, don't we?"

"I suppose we do," Sandy admitted doubtfully, "but somehow I don't think Mr. Miller would have looked at it that way at all."

When Lisa Carnaby came upstairs the next day to check on the summer models, Sandy was properly occupied with the walking shorts. Lisa seemed pleased.

"I'm glad Moffat has got you working on something useful," she said, looking over Sandy's shoulder. "Mr. Miller said something about a caftan, which is ridiculous. And he said you were draping on a model. He was delighted to see someone practicing the old craft." Her narrow smile suggested bored tolerance for her employer's foibles. "It's a waste of time, of course. I'm glad to see you at the drafting board. But surely Moffat should be doing this work."

"I'm just finishing it up for her."

Lisa frowned. "I suppose that's all right. You can't do too much damage by that. Where is Moffat?"

Sandy looked around the room, as if checking

the corners, then turned back to Lisa. "She doesn't seem to be here," she said helpfully.

Lisa gave a small twitch of annoyance. "I can see that for myself. Well, I can't spend any more time waiting for her. Tell her I came, and that I need those models—yesterday, if not sooner. This department is getting to be an absolute bottleneck."

Tracy stuck her face around the edge of the door as soon as Lisa had left. She was carrying the script. "Coast clear? I wondered if you would let me say my lines for you. I think I have them by heart."

Sandy glanced at the clock. "I suppose we could. This is supposed to be our lunch hour. Don't you want to go down to the cafeteria?"

"Never do," Tracy admitted. "My perfect weight wouldn't last long if I did. I bring my lunch: yogurt and rice cakes. Want to share?"

"Then there wouldn't be enough for you. Tell you what, I'll hear your lines now, and then you can run out and get me a cup of coffee and a doughnut."

"A doughnut!" Tracy's tone expressed deep envy. "Glazed maybe? Or chocolate frosted with colored-sugar sprinkles? I used to love those. Do you know how long it's been since I had one? Five years. I've been monitoring every mouthful of food I eat for five long years."

"But it's worth it, isn't it? How many perfect eights are there?"

"And how many perfect doughnuts? Never mind. Just help me with my part, and I'll get you all the empty calories you want. I won't even nibble on the corner of the bag."

The script was safely out of sight, and Sandy was most properly employed with tracing paper and one of Mrs. Moffat's foundation patterns when the next visitor arrived.

"I'm looking for Sandra Childs. Are you . . . ? May I come in?" This woman was obviously not management. Only a secretary could get away with the graceless comfort of such a sweater. It flopped from the woman's shoulders, its empty sleeves adangle, held on by a chain with little clips at each shoulder.

"I'm Sandy Childs. Did you bring a message for Mrs. Moffat?"

"Oh, no," the woman said, blinking. "I came to see you. It's about the play."

"All the parts have been cast, but I'm sure we could use more help. We could ask Jason if he wants someone to understudy, you know, like a backup."

"Good heavens, can you see me as an actress?" The woman giggled uncomfortably. "I don't want to be in the play. I'm Jason's secretary, and he sent me for your drawings. He said you would know what he meant."

Sandy felt let down. Jason had sent his secretary rather than come himself. His office was on the same floor. It would have taken less time for him to come and see her than he had spent telling the secretary to do it.

"I suppose he's very busy," Sandy said.

"The buyers are in town," the woman agreed, surprised by Sandy's unhappy face. "Jason never even came in today. He just called to tell me to get these drawings from you and to take them to display. Something about finding out if they're going to be able to build all those things."

Suddenly everything was all right again. Sandy felt like whooping for joy.

"Then you'll just need the sketches we made for the scenery," she said, beaming at the surprised secretary. "I'm so glad you dropped in. It's been so nice meeting you. I hope you'll come back."

Jason's secretary went away, carrying a bundle of sketches and telling herself that Sandy Childs seemed to be a very nice, friendly sort of woman but just a little bit odd.

Chapter Ten

*J*ASON came in at the end of the day, wearing his executive uniform again and carrying the monstrous scarf. The tattered fringe trailed behind him.

"Buyers are a peculiar species," he announced, "who should be confined to their native habitat, wherever that is. And now it's feeding time at the zoo. Close up shop and step on it."

Sandy was getting used to these abrupt appearances.

"I was going to stay and work on the costumes," she replied mildly.

"Eat first, work later," he said. "I've heard horrid reports of your eating habits. Things get around, you know. The scandal's out in the open. Everyone's talking about it."

Sandy blinked. "What scandal?"

"One glazed doughnut for lunch. My secretary heard about that from someone in purchasing, who got the dope direct from the cafeteria.

You see, you can't get away with anything around here."

"But it really was an exceptionally healthy doughnut," Sandy assured him. "Stuffed with soy proteins, dry skim milk, and vitamin supplements."

"Did it taste bad?"

"No," Sandy admitted. "It was rather good. You should try health doughnuts sometime."

Jason shook his head reprovingly. "You were deceived. What they gave you was just an ordinary doughnut. The wholesome, vitamin-stuffed ones taste grimly virtuous."

"Why do people eat them, then?"

"To gain merit, of course. It's like racking up points. When you do something sleazy, you have to make up for it by performing noble deeds."

Sandy fell in with his mood. "Killing dragons, maybe, and rescuing maidens?"

"Precisely! And you can imagine how difficult that can get. Many a well-intentioned nose has been busted by a maiden who had no wish to be rescued."

"How very sad. And I don't suppose dragons are as easy to find as they were a few years ago."

"They are close to becoming an endangered species. It's this rage for dragon-skin boots that's responsible."

"I would never buy them," Sandy protested virtuously. "It's cruel to dragons, and besides that—they leak."

After sharing one of Joe's huge salads, they walked down to Public Square, Jason's scarf wrapped around both of them. It was warm and cozy inside this odd wrapping, and passers-by pointed and laughed at them.

"Now, that's what I call two people wrapped up in each other," a man staggering out of a bar crowed.

"That must be what they call the tie that binds," his companion chortled.

"Is there some special reason why we are walking this way?" Sandy asked as the two celebrants reeled away. "I have to get back to work."

"This is part of your work," Jason assured her, his breath warm against her cheek. "There's a window at Higbee's that I want you to see."

"Brae-Mill clothes?"

"No, something else. You'll understand when you see it."

Sandy was puzzled until they came to the window. Then she saw what he meant. The theme of the display, unsurprisingly, was cruise clothes. A ship's railing ran across the back, with a deep blue curtain behind it. There were the inevitable life buoys, rather more believable than the ones she had constructed for Mrs. Roberts, and two mannequins placed in the foreground. The male figure was darkly handsome, well muscled and tanned, but it was the female who caught the eye.

"They make them very lifelike, don't they?"

Sandy observed. "She looks—I mean, she could almost be—"

"It's Tracy all right," Jason agreed, laughing. "I got the shock of my life when I saw her this morning. I hadn't had my first cup of coffee yet. My eyes were still half shut, and suddenly I came on this."

"Do you think she posed for it?"

"I don't suppose so. But she has been photographed, and they do try to get real-looking faces, rather than the doll-from-outer-space look that was in a few years ago. Well, that's all I wanted to show you. Now we'll go back."

Sandy took one last look at the window. "It's not just the resemblance that caught your eye," she decided. "It's the stance."

They turned back, a complicated maneuver because of the scarf, and examined the window from this distance.

"Of course," he said at last. "That's it, the way she is standing on tiptoe, with her head thrown back."

"And the way she holds that towel across her shoulders with both hands," Sandy said. "That's been bothering me—the fastening for the cloak."

"You specified a satin ribbon."

Sandy nodded. "I thought it was all right, but then your secretary came in for the scenery sketches. . . ."

"Mrs. Bond," he said, "a woman of many talents. She files things and is actually able to locate them again later."

"A splendid talent," Sandy agreed, "and she seems very nice, but she's not what you'd call a fashion plate, is she?"

Jason grinned. "Plain and wholesome is the term that comes to mind, or just plain dowdy. Do you want to design a new wardrobe for her?"

Sandy refused to be sidetracked. "It was her sweater that gave me second thoughts about Cindy's cloak. You know that little chain that keeps it from slipping off her shoulders?"

"Very functional. It leaves her arms free for useful stuff like filing, and gives the sweater that devastating sag across her back. I never gave it much thought, but you're right. It's a remarkable effect."

"That's it. Cindy can't have her cloak dragged across her shoulders and sagging down her back. It has to be held in position."

"Dabs of glue," Jason suggested. "I don't think Deb would let us use thumbtacks."

"That towel just seemed to float behind the girl in the window display, didn't it?"

He hugged her, excited. "I see what you're getting at."

She had to skip to keep up with his lengthening stride. "Hey, slow down. My legs are shorter than yours. But that's what I thought. Cindy could appear with her hands already raised, holding the cloak. She might have started unfastening it as she arrived at the White House."

"Of course. She knows she's late, and she starts unbuttoning herself."

"So by the time she steps into that archway, she is merely holding the cloak in her fingertips."

Jason was almost shouting with excitement. "Now we have movement. Bless you, Sandra Childs. Our Cindy does not have to stalk onstage, uncloak herself, then freeze for effect. She can come flying in, thoughtlessly letting go of her wrap as she moves downstage, so that it floats away behind her. We may have to use a fan to make sure it doesn't flop down around her feet and trip her up. She stops at the top of the stairs, because she is out of breath, and then floats slowly down into John's arms."

"Oh, yes," Sandy agreed.

"Like this," Jason said, holding her tight. "This is the way it must be."

They never did get back to work on the designs. There was too much to talk about, and the night was marvelously dry and crisp, perfect walking weather. They walked the twelve blocks to Theater Square and admired the restored movie palaces.

"Someday," Jason said dreamily, "we might put on a play at one of these."

"A gala performance," Sandy added, "with a

champagne supper served in the foyer for the patrons. I've read about those."

"No champagne for your everyday, common sort of patron," he corrected her. "Only the founding fathers, the ones who kicked in a thousand dollars or more. They get the lukewarm champagne and the leathery little sandwiches. It's popcorn and jug wine for the peasants."

"Are there really people who give that much money?"

"You bet. My grandfather is one of them."

Sandy was puzzled. "I had no idea he was interested in theater. I met him only once, of course, but he did seem so . . . practical, you know, and serious."

"Grandpa's interest in the theater," Jason explained with wry amusement, "is about as sincere as his love for the IRS. It was a tax write-off, Sandy. Grandpa is more than just practical and serious. He is a miserable skinflint, with a cashbox where his heart's supposed to be. Let's get back. It's getting colder."

Silent and moody, he drove her home. Sandy tried to cheer him up by talking, first about the play and then about her attempt to get out the samples. His answers were brief and polite. Not until they reached her place did he manage to shake off his gloom.

"I'm sorry," he said, holding the door for her. "Now and again it hits me from left field, that I gave up something I loved so much, and for what? To please an old man who doesn't care whether I live or die."

"Your grandfather must love you," Sandy protested. "He went to so much trouble to get you to come back."

"Grandfather will go to any amount of trouble to get his own way. As for love, he wouldn't recognize it if he tripped over it. Let's not talk about him. I get ugly when I think about him too much, and I've spoiled our evening together."

"No, you haven't," Sandy said softly. "Not unless you want to spoil it now. You sort of slowed it down, that's all. Would you like to come in for a while?"

"Are you offering me a rare cognac on the bearskin rug in front of a roaring fire?" Jason produced a marvelously silly, theatrical leer.

"No bearskin rug," Sandy admitted, "no cognac, and no fireplace. But we could have hot cocoa on Meg's plastic-topped coffee table. And if you feel you must have a fire, I suppose we could burn a few paper towels in the big ashtray."

"Sounds good," Jason decided. "I hope you have marshmallows."

They lit two of the stubby candles that Meg kept on hand for power failures, drank cocoa, and roasted marshmallows speared on toothpicks. Meg, coming in half an hour later, found them side by side on their knees in front of the coffee table, trying to clean up a mess of burnt sugar and candle drippings.

She shook her head at them. "I won't ask you what you've been doing. I don't think I want to know. But if you really want to get that goo off my table, you'd better get a sharp knife and a tub of hot water."

"I know we made a mess." Sandy was apologetic. "You see, we were trying to—all right, I won't tell you. I'll clean it up tomorrow morning, I promise."

Meg shrugged. "I've always hated that table. I paid ten dollars for it at a rummage sale, and I think I got stung. Next garbage day it goes out on the tree lawn. Aren't you going to introduce your friend?"

Sandy stumbled through the introductions, and Meg supervised the removal of the ruined table to the hallway leading to the staircase.

"Maybe someone will come along during the night and steal it," Meg said hopefully. "Doesn't the living room look great without it?"

They all went back into the apartment and drank more cocoa, while Meg questioned them about the progress of the play and shared a few insights into the real-estate business. Then the conversation got around to cars, since Meg was thinking of trading up to something better and Jason had just bought his Civic. In the middle of a discussion of rear- versus front-wheel drives, Meg got an idea.

"Why don't you drive Sandy home?" she asked Jason.

Jason blinked. "I thought that's what I did. Didn't I?"

"Not home here. Home to Pottersville. Didn't she tell you about the family reunion?"

"No," Jason said slowly. "She didn't."

"It's after dress rehearsal," Sandy assured him. "It won't interfere with my work."

Meg cast an exasperated glance in Sandy's direction. "That girl has no eye for opportunity. I hate to think what would happen to her if I weren't looking out for her. Her folks are expecting her, and she is just about ready to thumb her way to Pottersville."

"Don't," Sandy protested, blushing.

Jason regarded her with admiration, then turned to Meg. "Have you noticed that the girl can turn a beautiful rosy pink? I don't know anyone else who does that. Of course I'll take her home, if she promises to steer me. I'm told that Pottersville is hard to find, always getting lost in the folds of the map."

"But you don't have time," Sandy began. "I can't—"

"He has time and you can," Meg said firmly. "Will you please stop creating problems? The man just said he would take you, and your Aunt Kate will put him up in one of her guest rooms."

"I'm sure there's a motel where I could stay," Jason protested.

"Pottersville has a motel," Sandy admitted, "or at least it used to. No one has tried to stay there since 1953. It has tiny little cabins arranged in a circle around a woodsy-looking plumbing facility, and the sign says: 'One dollar per night.' "

"I'll accept your Aunt Kate's hospitality," Jason decided. "Shall we go straight from work on Friday, or would you rather leave on Saturday morning?"

"Saturday. I'm not sure anyone can find Pottersville in the dark. Even in daylight, it's important not to blink your eyes or sneeze. It's not what you'd call a metropolis. The business district is one gas pump and the post office."

"You're forgetting the motel," Jason reminded her.

"That's out of town, in the middle of our beautiful suburbs. There are cow pastures on either side."

"I can hardly wait." Jason looked very happy. "This is one aspect of America I've never seen. Good night, ladies. I'm going to leave you now. I shall also take the coffee table with me, and leave it on someone else's tree lawn. Meg, it's been a pleasure meeting you. Sandy, I'll see you tomorrow."

Meg stared after him when he left, and then she whistled. "So that's what you've been doing. Why didn't you tell me? He's gorgeous."

"I did tell you, remember? Jason's the man

who walked into Sew Nice looking for a designer, and he got me the job at Brae-Mill."

"Yeah, I know. You're also designing costumes for him. But you did not tell me that he was in love with you, not to mention vice versa."

Sandy was idiotically pleased by Meg's assumption, but felt she had to straighten her out. "There's nothing like that between us. We're just friends."

"Right," Meg agreed. "Just friends. And you just bought the Terminal Tower, right? Who do you think you're kidding?"

"Jason has never said anything about love," Sandy protested uncertainly.

Meg slapped her hand against her forehead. "Heaven grant me patience. Do you need a blueprint? That man is in love with you. His eyes follow you around every minute. He's happy just being in the same room with you. What do you want from him? A declaration of passion on bended knees?"

"That would be rather nice," Sandy said in a small voice.

"He looks just crazy enough to do that," Meg decided. "Show him to your folks. Get their approval, and on the way back you'll get your proposal—although bended knees are tricky inside a moving car. You may have to wait for a pit stop."

Chapter Eleven

*M*RS. Moffat came back and threw out most of Sandy's work.

"You did better than I had any right to expect," she said with a sigh. "Mr. Miller's right. I can't handle it all by myself. I'll have to let them hire a backup, at least one capable cutter who could hold the fort if I were to really get sick. Although next fall I will remember to get those flu shots, and you'll be able to handle the bulk of my work in a year or two. You did amazingly well."

Sandy felt let down. She had, after all, worked very hard, and had even fooled Mr. Miller into accepting her as a professional.

"Don't feel bad," Mrs. Moffat said kindly. "You did better than I would have done at your age. But look here, I won't have time to work with you for the next week or two, and the sample room is well staffed now. I'm glad we have Tracy. She fits in nicely. She can do a bit of everything, and—I don't care what they say—one live model is worth more than a dozen foundation patterns when you are working out a new design. Just concentrate on the costumes for Jason's play. It'll be marvelous training for you. You can do the whole thing, from first draft to final product. It's amazing what you learn from doing just that, and nowadays we don't often get the chance. Someone is forever taking the job away from you and giving it to a machine. So run along and have fun."

The next three weeks with their rush of work and rehearsals were fun, especially now that Sandy had the weekend trip to look forward to, knowing Jason wanted to meet her family. She didn't seriously accept Meg's idiotically romantic scenario, but neither could she dismiss it entirely. Whatever might happen on the way home, the prospect of the weekend in Pottersville opened up a whole world of pleasant daydreams. Even as she worked, Sandy found herself floating off into all sorts of lovely fantasies.

One afternoon Lisa Carnaby intruded on a particularly delightful daydream in which Sandy was skimming across the old skating pond with Jason's arms around her.

"I hope I am not disturbing you?" she inquired, giving the pile of theater sketches a quick, contemptuous glance.

Sandy laid down her pencil and wrestled her

mind back to the here and now. "I have permission to do this."

Lisa laughed tolerantly. "I didn't mean to panic you. Of course you're allowed to work on your own little sketches. Only, it's lunchtime, and I wondered if you wouldn't like to have a snack with me rather than face that awful cafeteria food. My treat."

Sandy had no special desire to lunch with Lisa, but neither could she think up a good excuse, so she thanked her politely and got her coat.

The snack, it turned out, was an extravagant salad plate at an elegant little restaurant just off the Square.

"I've been wanting to talk to you," Lisa announced, rearranging her salad in a way that reminded Sandy of Jason's technique for not eating. "Jason said something about your expecting him to drive you home this weekend."

Sandy felt chilled to the bone. "Is there any reason why he shouldn't?" she asked carefully.

"Several, I'd say." Lisa's voice was cool and light. "For one thing, it interferes with plans he and I made some time ago, and for another—I may be a bit old-fashioned, but I don't quite approve of a man going off for the weekend with anyone other than his fiancée. Do you?"

Sandy tried to say something and found that her voice was gone, completely gone, along with the fantasies, the joy, that lovely certainty that had enwrapped her like a soft blanket.

Lisa clucked her tongue impatiently. "He didn't tell you? That's really too bad of him. But he does like to play Santa Claus and make everyone happy."

"Jason is kind," Sandy agreed through stiff lips. "It was certainly very kind of him to offer to drive me home."

"The decent, sensible thing would have have been to give you money to rent a car," Lisa said with an air of irritated pity. "I'm not saying he meant any harm, but I don't think he ever gave a single thought to how you might interpret his offer. The trouble with Jason is that he has spent far too much time with people who express a lot of emotion without feeling it."

Sandy didn't want to believe Lisa, but her description of the way theater people behaved was fair enough.

Lisa warmed to the subject. "These people are forever calling each other darling. It's all hug-hug, kiss-kiss, and it doesn't mean a thing. I'm sure Jason had no idea you'd take him up on that crazy offer, and now, of course, he doesn't know how to get out of it." She gave a little laugh. "I can just see myself going through life, apologizing for him."

At last Sandy's voice was under partial control. "There's no need to apologize," she said quietly. "I'll tell him I changed my mind and don't have time to go."

Lisa gave her an encouraging nod. "I think

you're behaving just beautifully about this. I only hope it makes Jason realize how thoughtless he was." She tilted her head to one side. "But then again, he's not altogether to blame, is he now?" Sandy raised her head and met two cool, mocking eyes. Lisa's smile had become almost too bright. "You know what I'm talking about, don't you? What with the heady excitement of his theater project, and your puppylike devotion. . . . I suppose it was too much for him. He takes his games so very seriously."

Sandy was finally getting angry. "The play is not exactly a game," she protested. "Jason is serious about that."

Lisa's eyebrows rose, delicately ironic. "His play? *The Cinderella Game?* Is that something a grown-up can take seriously? Oh, you poor thing, you really do take it seriously, don't you?"

The lovely daydreams about Jason had dissolved into thin air, and Sandy needed something to hang on to. Surely some part of her happiness was based on reality.

"Maybe it's not a serious play," she insisted, "but I think it is going to be good entertainment, well produced and fun to watch. The audience will have a good time."

"Maybe." Lisa had stopped smiling. "Audiences are easy to amuse. Look at what passes for prime-time entertainment. But I wasn't thinking of the show. I was thinking of the Cinderella game that you've been playing."

"I haven't been—"

"Of course you have, whether you realized it or not." Lisa's beautiful mouth twitched contemptuously. "It's a cute game. Poor little girl from the wrong side of the tracks meets the boy who has everything. Stars form in her eyes. Light bulbs switch on in her head. It's romance with a capital *R*. He wines and dines her, a cardboard moon overhead and muted violins in the background. Finally the big moment: He pulls her into his manly arms and kisses her upturned face. The violins rise to a passionate crescendo and the lights fade out. Wow!"

Sandy got to her feet, willing her knees not to shake. "I'd better get back to work," she said.

"Much better," Lisa agreed contemptuously. "Because that's as far as the game goes, isn't it? The trouble with your Cinderella game is that it doesn't work. When the lights go on again, the prince is back home with a suitable sort of princess vetted by the government and approved by the press. Cinderellas have a rotten time of it these days. I suspect they always did."

"Thank you for lunch," Sandy said stiffly.

Lisa was all smiles again. "We must do this again sometime," she murmured. "Don't forget what I said. It's meant for your own good. Find another game for yourself, Sandy, one you have a chance of winning."

*   *   *

Sandy had no idea how she got back to work.

"You look awful," Mrs. Moffat said. "I hope you haven't caught my bug. Jason popped in while you were out to lunch. Better give him a call."

Sandy picked up the phone. "Mrs. Bond? No, I don't need to speak to Jason. Just give him a message. There's a change in my plans. I'm not going out of town this weekend."

Mrs. Bond was still assuring her that Sandy could tell Jason herself, when Sandy quietly put down the receiver.

Two minutes later, he exploded into the room. "What's going on?" he demanded. "Do you realize I actually bought snow tires just for this trip? You can't brush me off without an explanation, not after I made an investment like that."

Sandy refused to go along with his mood. "Let's forget the whole thing. Okay?"

Jason folded his arms across his chest. "What made you change your mind? I think I have a right to know."

Mrs. Moffat got up. "If you two are going to argue," she protested, "I'm going down for a cup of tea. I'll be gone ten minutes, and I want this room quiet and peaceful when I get back."

Jason waited until the door closed behind her, then tried to pull Sandy into his arms. "Now tell me what this is all about."

She extricated herself and retreated behind a table. "I don't really have time to go home for the weekend," she said. "The dress rehearsal is almost here, and there are still a million things to be done. I've had an idea for Polly's ball gown. I want to work on that."

At first Jason looked as though he accepted what she said at face value. Then his eyes caught hers and she looked away. "All right," he said, "I agree—there are a million things to do. Maybe a trip this weekend isn't a good idea. But there's more to it than that, isn't there?"

"Lisa took me out to lunch," she said quietly. "She said you had other plans for the weekend."

"We were supposed to go to the opera benefit," Jason admitted. "But she could easily find someone else to go with."

"She also mentioned that you were engaged to her."

Jason looked stunned.

Sandy clenched her fists to stop herself from shaking. "Did you want to keep it a secret?"

"Some secret!" Jason said, and he whirled around and rushed out of the office.

Sandy watched him go, suddenly realizing how desperately she had been waiting for him to tell her that there was no engagement. The last sliver of her golden daydream crumbled into dust.

When Mrs. Moffat came back a few minutes later, Sandy sat hunched, staring intently at her drawing board. Mrs. Moffat thought that somewhat odd, because the paper was completely blank.

Calling home to explain that she wasn't coming was no fun. Telling Meg was worse. Meg had her own investment in the Jason fantasy and felt guilty as well as disappointed.

"Don't look at me that way," Meg begged. "I really thought. . . . And I still say he's in love with you. He could have ten fiancées, each one more gorgeous than the next, but on the basis of how he looks at you, my guess would still be the same. That man is in love with you."

"He's in love with Lisa." Sandy tried hard to sound quietly matter-of-fact. "He must be if he asked her to marry him."

"*If* he did, it was temporary insanity," Meg suggested.

Sandy heaved a sigh. "She's a very sane choice. She'll help him adjust to the realities of life. She comes across as a very practical sort of woman."

"A useful quality," Meg agreed, "but not one that necessarily inspires guys with mad passion."

Sandy tried to be fair. "She is also very beautiful, tall and thin, a perfect fashion plate. For someone in his position, a wife like that. . . . And she understands the business. She'll be able to help him."

"You've given me several reasons why he

should give her a raise," Meg snapped, "and not one good reason why he should marry her."

"Well, he is going to marry her." Sandy forced a smile. "I'm sorry, Meg. I wish things would work out the way you think they should."

"I have awfully good ideas," Meg agreed mournfully. "I think your friend Jason should be in love with you because the two of you make such a nice couple. And I think Al should grow up and decide to settle down, because I'm going to have to start looking for someone else if he doesn't. For a woman with such a lot of splendid ideas, I'm not doing so good." She regarded Sandy anxiously. "How bad is it?"

"I'm getting over it already." It sounded so good that for a moment Sandy almost believed it herself. "Now that I know. . . . You see, Meg, he's just one of those people who can't help being charming. He's so vital, interested in everything and everybody. And that business of hugging and kissing—he kisses all the women, even Susan, who's pushing retirement age, and he throws his arms around everyone, the men just as much as the women. It's just a friendly mannerism. I built up a fantasy, that's all."

"I could have sworn that man was in love with you." Meg sighed. "It's that marvelous intuition of mine, that same intuition that encouraged me to pin all my hopes for the future on one Al Patterson."

"You don't have to give up on Al," Sandy

said, trying to rally her. "You have almost two years left."

Meg's lips trembled. "Who needs two more years of torture? I'm getting lockjaw from smiling, when I really want to hang myself around his neck and scream at him that I'm tired of his so-called good times and would like a bit of reality for a change."

"Is it that bad?"

"Bad enough," Meg said with a sigh. "Maybe you're lucky after all—a clean break, no messy unfinished business."

Chapter Twelve

*I*N a way, Jason made it easy for Sandy, because he treated her with the same friendliness he extended to everyone.

Sandy wished she could match his amiable detachment. She had spent a lonely, miserable weekend, and it was hard for her to pretend everything was all right. She tried to be relaxed and cheerful, but Mrs. Moffat immediately noticed something was wrong.

"You've caught my disease," she prophesied. "You look the way I felt just before I came down with it. Why don't you go home?"

"Because dress rehearsal's the day after tomorrow," Sandy explained wearily. "I'm meeting with Cal Rosen from display this afternoon to see what he's done with my drawings and to help his crew put the scenery in place. Then I still have to be on hand to prompt for the actual dress rehearsal. After that I can get as sick as I want."

* * *

The scenery was nailed and lashed into place. It looked dull and shabby in the glare of the overhead lights. But then, everything looked dull and shabby to Sandy these days.

"Not to worry," Cal assured her. "Wait till you see it with the proper lights."

"What lights?" Sandy was not to be coaxed out of her gloom. "The supposed stage manager, Gus's friend Gloria, hasn't shown her face yet."

Gloria turned up half an hour before the dress rehearsal and took charge. She was a sturdy young woman in dusty black jeans and sweatshirt, armed with a huge clipboard and an air of authority. She examined the stage minutely, made some minor adjustments, and consulted a heavily marked script.

Finally she noticed Sandy. "Who are you?"

"Sandra Childs. Can I help?"

"Nice of you." Gloria did not seem thrilled by Sandy's offer. "You're not getting billing, are you? I was promised stage manager."

"My credit is for design," Sandy explained. "See, it says *Costumes by Brae-Mill* on the program. That's me."

"If that's all you want. . . ." Gloria decided that Sandy might be allowed to be useful after all. "Check the prop table against this list, will you? Make sure everything is in the right order."

Gus came early, a slumped, lackluster figure carrying a bundle of radio scripts.

"So you finally made it," he hissed at Gloria. "Did you at least get the cue sheet from Jason?"

"Everything's under control," Gloria snapped, calmly turning her back on him.

Gus grumbled quietly to himself and disappeared into the men's dressing room.

Susan came next, bringing a thermos jug of hot lemonade, and Tracy arrived, carrying her fold-up ironing board and a steam iron. Soon after that, George wheeled in the rack with the costumes, and with that, Sandy experienced a rising sense of excitement. The mere sight of the red dresses put her into a fever. Now it really was going to happen. All the separate parts were coming together—the scenery; the carefully prepared tapes; those troublesome lights that Gloria seemed to understand; the six actors, word perfect in their parts; and Sandy's costumes. Together these things would form the show.

Once the actors were dressed and made up, Polly was no longer a pleasant motherly figure, and Gus seemed to have lost twenty years and thirty pounds. Deb, her punk hairstyle covered by a flowing wig, looked demure and fragile.

Jason checked over the props, thanked Gloria for coming, and asked her if she needed an extra rehearsal for her cues.

"No need," she decided. "The only tricky parts are in the third act. If I don't get those right tonight, then maybe I will need a technical run-through later on."

Jason then turned to Sandy. "You'll prompt?" He seemed about to say something else, but didn't.

Sandy forced herself to smile. "They all know their lines."

Jason had become businesslike. "Sometimes that doesn't help. People have been known to dry up in a play they have done a hundred times. Just sit in the wings with the book. That's a good girl." He had said *girl,* not *woman,* and Sandy did not feel like joking about it.

Then Polly came up to her, fussing with the brim of her hat. "I'm not sure about this," she complained. "What did you have in mind?"

Sandy pulled the hat down and adjusted the brim. "Bella Abzug," she said.

Polly beamed. "Of course. Now I know how to wear it."

At the very last moment Tracy came down with another case of nerves.

"I've forgotten my cue," she wailed. "My mind's a complete blank."

"Sandy is holding the book," Jason reassured her. "She'll give you the cue. I want you to relax. Just remember that this is a rehearsal, no more. We can stop at any point and go back."

"But I've put so much work into it," Tracy protested tearfully. "I want to be perfect."

"Heaven forbid." Jason crossed his fingers. "Promise me at least one flub. A perfect dress rehearsal is the worst possible sign. It's ominous.

luck before a performance, or bringing an open
umbrella into the house. Let's hope and pray for
a rotten dress rehearsal. Let every single thing
go wrong tonight. That would mean that we have
a chance to put on a good performance three
days from now."

Sandy would think about that later. For the
next two hours, she was too busy to think at all.
Nobody dried up, not even Tracy, and it would
not have mattered if they did. Sandy realized
that she no longer had to consult the script. It
was all in her head. She could have supplied any
missing line from her memory. In fact, when Gus
paused dramatically at one point, she found herself hissing out his next line, and got a dirty look
for her pains.

Gloria handled the lights beautifully, even the
intricate sequence of cues in the third act. As
Deb came onstage, the balance began to shift im-
perceptibly. The lights and music emanating
from the ballroom receded, and simultaneously
Gloria raised the fader on the center flood, so
that Deb was bathed in a golden glow at the very
moment she arrived at the top of the steps. There
she stood poised, her fingertips barely touching
her shoulders. She was so beautiful, it took
Sandy's breath away. The fan in the wings
whirred gently, and the cloak drifted to the
ground behind her.

"Cindy," Gus said, his deep, manly voice filled

with emotion. "I was afraid you weren't coming. . . ."

And then it was over. Gloria switched off the lights, checked the prop table one last time, then grabbed her script.

"Now for the comments," she said. "Prepare to be blasted."

"But it went perfectly well," Sandy protested. "There were no flubs."

"No outright mistakes maybe, but some imperfections. Wait till you hear Jason lay into us."

Jason, however, laid into no one, not even Tracy for her precurtain hysteria. "It went almost too well," he announced. "Thank you all for a beautiful job. Polly, Gus, you're a joy to work with. I had forgotten how good you are. And, Susan, that was a small gem you turned in tonight. And Deb. . . . Where is Deb?"

Startled, they looked at one another, then looked around, as if a girl in a bright red dress were something that could get mislaid among eight people.

Polly was the first to locate her. "Deb's at the back of the house," she said, surprised. "She's talking to someone."

"Get her," Jason snapped. "I have a few notes for her."

Sandy jumped down from the stage and ran to where Deb was standing. Lisa was with her, along with an obtrusively well-dressed man with a glittering smile.

Not a theater person, was Sandy's mental note. *Too carefully dressed for that, and not in the clothing trade either. I wonder what he's doing here.*

Deb turned dreaming eyes to Sandy and tried to focus on her. "I am sorry. I should be onstage, I know, but something's come up."

"Jason has notes for you." Sandy had never seen Deb look so radiant.

"I'll have to talk to him, won't I?" Deb murmured dreamily. "You'll excuse me, Mr. Corcoran? It'll only take a minute or two."

She swirled up to the stage, the red gown billowing behind her, while Sandy followed more slowly, admiring the flowing lines of the red dress in motion.

"That was the wrong time to disappear." Jason sounded none too gracious. "Sit down, Deb. I'm going over the play, line by line. Your timing was off in places."

"I'm afraid I can't stay for the rehash." Deb's smile was bright and remote. "And it doesn't really matter, does it?"

Everyone stared at her, so that she became defensive.

"Well, something's come up, something important for me. I'm afraid I won't be able to do the show with you." She looked hopefully around at the circle of serious faces. "You understand, don't you?"

As if on cue, everybody stood up and moved

away from her. Sandy went with the rest. It was an attack of almost physical aversion. She simply wanted to get as far away from Deb as possible. She wondered if the others felt the same.

Only Jason stayed behind, facing Deb, his eyes narrowed. "May I ask what your present plans are?" he asked with careful courtesy.

Deb was too involved in blissful contemplation of her own affairs to catch the undertone of rage behind his tight-lipped smile. "Mr. Corcoran has offered me a job. You know—Mark Corcoran of Acme."

"Advertising?"

Deb nodded eagerly. "I guess everyone's heard of Acme. They're real big in New York and on the West Coast. Mr. Corcoran is wonderful."

"I can see from here that he is a very hip dresser," Jason said drily. "What sort of job is he offering you?"

"It's sweet of you to take an interest," Deb burbled, "especially since this means I have to drop out of your show. But I knew you'd understand. You've been so sweet. It's a road show, a musical."

Jason gave a quick, puzzled glance in the direction of the impeccable Mr. Corcoran, who was now deep in conversation with Lisa. "I thought you said he runs an advertising agency."

Deb was all aflutter. "Just about the biggest

in New York, and he's got the Chrysler account. Isn't that fabulous?"

"Quite," Jason agreed. "Where does your road show fit in?"

Deb's hands were clasped under her chin. Her eyes were shining. "It's a promo. We'll cover just about every city where Chryslers are sold—to hype up the salesmen, you see, get them excited about the new models."

Jason's rage drained out of him, leaving him sad-eyed. "Poor Deb," he said gently. "There's no future in that. It's a single shot. When it's over, you'll be right where you started. I hoped at least you were letting me down for something worthwhile."

His pity penetrated Deb's euphoria, where his anger had merely bounced off. "I'm sorry about leaving," she protested. "But we never signed anything, did we? You could just as easily have replaced me without warning." She was working herself up into a state of indignation. "You don't understand the ad game. This is important. It's my big chance, much too good to pass up. It's going to give me exposure, you see. It identifies me with the Chrysler product." Her eyes became soft and dreamy again. She was back on her pink cloud. "It could lead to almost anything, ads in the trade magazines and in the glossies. And commercials, prime-time commercials—all those residuals, imagine. Lisa says it's just a matter of getting your foot in the door."

Jason's eyes darkened. "You have discussed this with Lisa?"

Deb's eyes flew wide open. "Oh, didn't I tell you? It was her idea. She invited Mr. Corcoran to the dress rehearsal. I don't know how she happened to think of me being the right talent for the Chrysler promo campaign, but isn't it great of her, thinking of me and bringing Mr. Corcoran here to see me?"

"Just great," Jason said, his eyes fixed on Lisa. She was listening to Mr. Corcoran, her head bent forward, giving him that intent, undivided attention that buyers always found so flattering. "When did this first come up?"

"Does it matter?" Deb asked.

"I was wondering if you couldn't have warned me earlier on, so I could have rehearsed another Cynthia. Surely it must have occurred to you that it would be nice for me to be told ahead of time."

Deb became uneasy. "Oh, I see what you're getting at, but you can't blame me. I had no inkling of any of this. I had never even heard of Mr. Corcoran or the Chrysler account until tonight. Lisa kept it a secret. I guess she didn't want me to be nervous and ruin my chance. I didn't know a thing, not even that someone important was going to be watching the dress rehearsal."

"But Lisa knew," Jason said quietly. "How long has she known?"

"Four or five weeks, I imagine." Deb was no longer interested, now that she knew Jason was not blaming her. "She must have been working on it for more than a month. Mr. Corcoran says he met her in New York early in February and told her about the Chrysler campaign."

"About the time we started rehearsing," Jason murmured thoughtfully.

Deb, however, had caught Mr. Corcoran's eye and was anxious to get away. "Thank you for being so nice about it," she said, quickly kissing his cheek. "It's a shame about the play. I would have liked to stay for it, but Lisa says I mustn't start by asking for special treatment. I can't afford to inconvenience Mr. Corcoran, can I? But, Jason, I do adore this dress, and I think it's lucky for me. I don't suppose you would let me keep it?"

"We still have a show to put on," Jason reminded her coldly.

She blew him a kiss and ran off to gurgle her thanks to Mr. Corcoran. Jason stood quite still, watching her, his face a blank mask.

Sandy watched this exchange, stunned by the utter unfairness of it. They had all worked so hard to put the show together. It had been the only link left between her and Jason, and now it was gone, destroyed. She felt tired and sad.

Polly, on the other hand, became energetic. "Somebody has to talk to Jason," she decided.

"If we don't give him a chance to blow off steam, he's going to explode. I know him."

"What can we say?" Sandy protested unhappily.

"It doesn't matter what we say," Polly snapped. "He just needs a chance to talk. Come on."

She strode over to Jason, the reptile tail of her dress twitching. Sandy straggled behind her, still wondering what comfort anyone could offer.

"Don't blame the poor little airhead," Polly was saying. "It seems like a rotten thing to do, but it's hard to turn down an opportunity."

Jason turned to her, his eyes blazing. "Would you have done it?"

"I'm not sure. Maybe, if I thought it would turn my career around. . . ." Polly thought about it some more, then shook her head. "I guess I wouldn't, but not for any highfalutin moral reason. Look, Jason, I'm an established actress, and my reputation rests on the fact that I am reliable. If I were to let you down, it would soon get around, and the jobs would dry up. My Play House contract is safe enough, but the bread-and-butter jobs—the jingles, the voice-overs—no sensible producer stakes good studio time on someone who may or may not be there to finish the job."

"But if you could be sure no one would ever find out," Jason persisted. "Would you walk out on me?"

Polly smiled ruefully. "I don't suppose I would, but then I'm fond of you, and I love the play."

"And nobody has offered you an irresistible opportunity, such as a promo road show, to whip up a bunch of Chrysler dealers into feverish enthusiasm for their work." Jason's eyes glittered angrily. "Think of the possibilities: prime-time commercials, your face on every TV set across the nation, residuals, the works."

"Good stuff, all of it," Polly said soberly, "but it won't happen, and you know it. Deb and her road show will stay on the road until the campaign's over. Then they'll hire New York talent to do the commercials."

Jason turned to look at the group by the door. It was a classic tableau, perfect in its way. Deb was going through her paces for Mr. Corcoran. Her eyes sparkled, her hands fluttered, and her head was tilted back to show off her lovely long neck. Mr. Corcoran was looking heavily handsome and amiable. It was Lisa, however, who riveted the eye.

"Perfect casting," Polly murmured dreamily. "The hero, the heroine, and the heroine's confidante. Every play needs one. She can be a nurse, a friend, or a maiden aunt. She moves the plot along and helps the principals achieve their heart's desire. And just look at that lovely attitude, self-effacing and concerned. I don't know who that woman is, but she's terrific."

Jason's eyes had become thoughtful. "You're right," he said. "I have underestimated Lisa's talents."

Chapter Thirteen

*C*AL Rosen, the man from Display, drove Sandy home. He was silent, making no attempt to cheer her up, and she was grateful for that.

"Rotten bad luck," he finally said, holding the door for her. "I've gotten fond of the show. We all have. But, who knows, something may still turn up."

Sandy wanted to hang on to that. "Jason knows a lot of actors, and there are three days left. Maybe he'll find someone for the part."

"Right you are," Cal agreed, but he did not sound as if he believed it.

Meg was waiting for her, very bright eyed and excited. "Well, how was dress rehearsal?"

"It went off without a hitch," Sandy said with a sigh. "Jason said something before we started, that a perfect rehearsal is unlucky. I didn't think much about it at the time."

"Something went wrong afterward? Something serious?"

173

"You might say that," Sandy agreed drily. "Our leading lady walked out on us."

"She quit?" Meg was puzzled. "She and Jason had a fight?"

"No. Someone offered her a better job." Sandy found that she didn't want to talk about it. "Do we have enough milk to make cocoa?"

Meg's smile was crooked, secretive. "No cocoa tonight. We drink wine to celebrate."

"Celebrate dress rehearsal?" Sandy was puzzled. There was something odd about Meg's expression. "Or is there something else?"

In answer, Meg held out her left hand. The ring was simple. The diamond was small. But Meg's eyes made up for whatever it lacked.

Sandy was amazed. "Al proposed tonight?"

Meg picked up a pillow and hugged it to her chest. "Nothing that romantic. He called me at work and said our date was off, that the ring had cost a lot more than he expected and he simply couldn't afford to take me out. So I told him that I'd provide the dinner, since he was paying for the ring. I picked up a couple of steaks on the way home, and he brought two bottles of wine. We drank one, and I took away his car keys and made him walk home. It's only five blocks, and I have an investment to protect. I can't let him kill himself now."

Sandy forgot all about her own troubles. "Oh, Meg, I'm so happy for you."

Meg's eyes were like stars. "Seems he's been

thinking about it ever since he got a raise in January. He picked out the ring, but it ended up costing more than he expected, and he got into a panic."

"But it's all right now?"

Meg hugged her pillow. "It's better than all right. It's great. You know, all that talk about ditching Al and looking for someone willing to settle down—that was whistling in the dark. I couldn't have done it. I guess it's always been Al, always will be." Then she remembered Sandy's situation and tried hard to subdue her exuberance. "Am I making things worse for you? Would you rather I shut up?"

"No," Sandy said softly. "It's wonderful seeing you happy. It proves that sometimes things do work out the way we want them to. Did you say some of the wine was left? I want to drink a toast to you and Al."

The sample room was buzzing with news of the disaster. The only one who took no interest was Mrs. Moffat, who was still trying to make up the time she had lost to her bout with the flu. Everyone else talked about the dress rehearsal. The consensus was that Jason would probably give up on these theater projects, seeing how easily they could go sour.

Sandy decided wearily that that might be just as well. Since Lisa seemed to have such strong objections to Jason's theater work, perhaps he should give it up rather than have it become a permanent bone of contention between them. Certainly Lisa had been underhanded in the way she had sabotaged Jason's play, but Sandy was coming to the depressing conclusion that Jason was just as devious. Look at the way he had manipulated her. Those two, she concluded bitterly, deserved each other.

The best cure for disappointment, she decided, was work. She settled down to the unalluring job of tracing foundation patterns, something she had been putting off. It needed to be done, but it was exacting and dull.

She was bent over the drawing board when Mrs. Bond burst into the room. Jason's secretary looked awful. The dowdy sweater was dragged across her shoulders more tightly than usual. Her eyes were swollen, and she had a handkerchief clutched to her nose.

"Can I stay here for a few minutes?" she begged tearfully. "I'll be all right in a while, but I don't want to go to the cloakroom or the cafeteria. I don't want anyone to see me until I've stopped shaking."

Mrs. Moffat was irritated. "Have you considered going down to see the nurse?"

"I'm not sick." Mrs. Bond looked miserable. "It's so unpleasant. I don't know what to do."

Mrs. Moffat gave her a closer look. "You look bad," she admitted. "Sandy, do we still have that electric hot pot? Mrs. Bond needs a cup of coffee."

"That might help." Mrs. Bond collapsed into a chair and struggled to get hold of herself. "It's so unexpected, you see. Jason has always been so nice. I've never seen him like this."

"What did he do?" Sandy couldn't imagine Jason's being rude to his secretary. He might be sleazy in his personal relationships, but he was always nice to the people who worked for him.

Mrs. Bond held her cup of instant coffee to her temples. "That helps—the heat, you know. I should have seen this coming. Jason was quite short with me this morning, and that's not like him. I thought he might still be upset about that actress. But then Lisa Carnaby came in, and he started shouting at her, really shouting. He called her some terrible names. You wouldn't believe the language. . . ."

Mrs. Moffat, however, had had enough. "Finish your coffee and go," she said crisply. "I don't have time for gossip. Pull yourself together."

"Yes, of course," Mrs. Bond said humbly. "I didn't mean. . . . The coffee was just what I needed. Thank you."

"That woman's a nuisance," Mrs. Moffat growled. "On the other hand, Jason should know better than to mix business and social life. I knew there'd be trouble when he started dating Lisa. I hope nobody else overheard the ruckus."

As it turned out, however, Jason's harangue

had been overheard by one other person. Tracy buttonholed Sandy and asked her in a hushed voice if she had heard.

"Heard what?" Sandy asked cautiously.

"Jason yelling at the top of his lungs. He blames Lisa for Deb's walking out on him, and she certainly didn't help smooth things down. You should have heard her."

Sandy wondered if she should try to stop these confidences, but nothing could have stopped Tracy. She was bursting to tell.

"It was awful. Jason was boiling mad and Lisa got more and more amused. She was laughing at him, telling him he was a dope to get so upset over his silly old play. She didn't actually use those words, but that's what came across."

"She was laughing?" There was a sharp pain in Sandy's chest. "How could she?"

"Lisa disapproves of the plays," Tracy said glumly. "She thinks they're a dumb waste of time. What I don't understand is that she would talk to him that way. I mean, he's her boss."

"He is also her fiancé."

"Honest?" Tracy looked amazed, then doubtful. "Are you sure? They may have been engaged last night, but I don't think they are anymore, not after that fight."

"People say things they don't mean. You'll have to pretend you didn't hear anything. Okay?"

Tracy shrugged. "I can try. If you mean I

shouldn't gossip, don't worry. I have better things to do. Aren't you going to ask me why I was standing outside Jason's door, listening?"

"I'm not interested," Sandy said firmly. "I don't want to know."

Tracy looked disappointed. "I wanted to tell someone, and I couldn't very well talk to Jason while he was yelling. I've been up half the night, learning the lines, and now nobody wants to listen to me."

"What lines?" Finally Sandy was paying attention.

Tracy saw that she had found her audience. "I know Deb's part," she confided triumphantly. "I can play Cindy. I know I can. Do you think Jason will let me try?"

"Let's go and ask him," Sandy suggested.

Jason's office showed no sign of upheaval. Mrs. Bond was crouched over her typewriter, stabbing away at the keys, and the door to the inner office was ajar.

"I don't know if Jason will see anyone this morning," the secretary started doubtfully.

"He'll see us," Sandy said firmly.

Jason looked tired, but he welcomed them pleasantly enough and asked them to sit.

Tracy perched on the very edge of the chair, as if poised to take off and soar. "It's about the play."

"I'm sorry about that," Jason said quietly. "I

know how hard you worked on it. I've been calling around, trying to find someone who can step in and play Cindy. Right now it doesn't look too hopeful. We may have to scrap the show."

Tracy could no longer contain herself. "But I can play Deb's part, really. I know all the lines. I stayed up all night learning them."

Jason leaned forward, examining Tracy through narrowed eyes. "How about the movements?" he snapped.

Tracy laughed joyously. "That part's easy. I always remember movements. It was the lines I wasn't sure of. But Sandy gave me some tips on learning lines. I know them. I can read them for you."

"Let's go, then." Jason had stopped looking tired. "Where's the script? Someone has to give you your cues."

"I can do that," Sandy offered. "I know all the parts."

"You do? All six parts? Cynthia's too?"

"Only the words," Sandy admitted. "I wouldn't be able to play the parts, but I can give Tracy her cues."

An hour later, Jason sent a bewildered Mrs. Bond out for coffee and sandwiches. Still later, he appeared in the outer office, tieless, rumpled, and grinning.

"Mrs. Bond," he said, "stop whatever you're doing. Contact everyone involved in *The Cinderella Game.* If you have trouble getting hold of the pros, call the schools and the recording studios. Don't let them brush you off. We have to work fast. Special rehearsal tonight."

Polly was less than amiable about this sudden call. "I'm willing to try anything for your sake, but this is crazy."

Nothing could bring Jason down. "Crazy perhaps," he agreed cheerfully. "But it's going to work. I know it will."

"I can see several minor problems already." Polly was sour at having been dragged out on a nasty night. "Let's assume Tracy really can step into Deb's part. Who's going to play hers?"

"No problem. Sandy will play Miss Brown. She doesn't know it yet, but she will."

"I can't act," Sandy protested. "I know the lines, but I can't play a part."

"You can and you will," Jason informed her, grinning. "Get into costume. Polly will help you with makeup."

Gus was grumpy and walked limply through his part, speaking the lines in his thinnest, most fretful squeak. Susan was flustered. Gary and George struggled to adjust to the change in the play. Part of the time, they forgot and stood around looking for Deb instead of speaking their lines to Tracy. The only one pleased by the extra rehearsal was Gloria, who paid no attention to the actors at all, except to make certain that they had the correct lighting at any given moment.

At last it was over.

"If you want another surprise rehearsal," Gus huffed, "you can find a stand-in for me."

"We don't need another rehearsal," Jason assured him. "The curtain goes up as planned, ready or not."

"I would prefer ready." Polly was tired and glum. "But then again, why should I care? I have nothing to lose but my reputation."

In answer, Jason gave her a bear hug, and she went away chuckling to herself.

He then turned to Sandy. "Haven't you got your coat on yet? Good heavens, woman, must you always keep me waiting? Of course I'm driving you home. Did you expect me to stake you a taxi again? Do you think I'm made of money?"

Sandy made no attempt to sort out her feelings. It was as if the world had tilted, putting them back where they had started. They were strangers again, alone together for the first time. She would not permit herself to be happy; she hardly dared to breathe. It meant nothing. He was just being friendly, driving her home.

Instead of driving southeast, however, Jason drove north to the Shoreway, then turned west.

"Lakewood," he explained, "a gracious suburb filled with well-maintained houses, neatly landscaped. You'll like it."

Sandy didn't know whether to laugh or cry.

"I've heard a lot of good stuff about Lakewood," she admitted. "Why are you taking me there?"

He pulled the car off the road so suddenly that she fell against his shoulder. "Hey," she started to protest, but got no further, because he was kissing her.

"We're going to see Grandpa and tell him that we're getting married." Jason sounded enormously pleased with himself. "It's only fair to tell him. It doesn't matter if he disapproves, but we'll give him a chance to be nice about it."

"But—"

"You do talk a lot, don't you? Can't you let me have my say? Lisa told me that I talk nonsense, so I'll try and keep it simple. I love you. I'm sure you knew that all along."

"But—"

"Lisa told you we were engaged, but you must have known that was nonsense. We went out a few times, that's all. The engagement was a figment of her imagination."

"I asked you," Sandy protested. "I asked you straight out and you didn't deny it."

He looked astounded. "What do you mean? Of course I denied it!"

"No, you didn't. I asked if you had wanted to keep your engagement a secret, and you said, 'Some secret!' and stormed out of the room."

"So?" he asked, spreading his hands as if that explained everything.

"So, I thought you were mad because Lisa had let the secret out of the bag."

"Oh, no!" He shook his head in amazement. "What I meant was that the engagement was a secret even from me. I thought you understood. You knew I was in love with you, so how could I be engaged to Lisa? I rushed out of there to find out what was going on. Before I got to Lisa's office, I was hit with another thought. Maybe she had taken our few casual dates too seriously. Maybe she had fallen in love with me and somehow really thought we were engaged—I have this dumb tendency to associate engagements with love." He grinned ruefully. "I wanted to be a gentleman and let her down gently. I didn't want to hurt her feelings, but it turns out her feelings were never involved. I was supposed to give her a hand up the corporate ladder." He shrugged. "Our imaginary engagement was dissolved by mutual agreement, except there was nothing agreeable about it."

"But if you were never engaged. . . ."

"Lisa's not the type to let small things like reality stand between her and her plans." Jason's tone was dry, amused. "I was handpicked to further her career. So we had a glorious, no-holds-barred fight, and after that there was no more talk of an engagement. I'm slime as far as she's concerned. I'm also free as air. Will you marry me?"

Sandy's head was spinning. "You're crazy,"

she gasped. "We hardly know each other, and your grandfather will have a fit."

"I've made a few mistakes in my life," Jason said thoughtfully. "Dating Lisa was one of them, and letting Grandpa bully me was another. He wants me in the business? Fine. I'm in, and I think I'm beginning to enjoy it."

"But the theater?"

He hugged her. "We'll always have that, love, and not just as a hobby. Don't you realize what a marvelous showcase such a performance can be for the clothes you design? If Chrysler can build a show to tout their product, so can Brae-Mill. Hey, you didn't really think I'd let you sit at home getting fat and lazy, did you? I need you in the business. That's one of the things we're going to tell Grandpa. I want you to design a new line, fantasy clothes—back to the sixties. I think the world's ready for it."

"But—"

"I never knew such a woman for gabbing. Can't you listen for once? You don't want to leave our children at home with strangers, right? Not to worry. I've been thinking about opening up a day nursery for our workers. Grandpa's had women working for him all his life, and never once has he taken an interest in their problems. We're going to do better. Together, you and I can turn that old plant into something wonderful. Okay. I'm finished. Your turn."

Sandy felt swept along so fast that she could

hardly breathe. "You're rushing things," she complained desperately. "I need time to think. I need to get to know you better before we make long-range plans. This is too serious to rush."

"I'll give you time to make up your mind," Jason declared. "It's rather generous of me, but I warn you—after ten years, the deal's off." Suddenly there was a desperate note of sincerity under the lightness. "I am quite painfully in love with you, so if you could make an effort to think this through a bit faster, I'd be much obliged."

Sandy's heart was doing acrobatics inside her rib cage. "You fool," she whispered. "You know that I love you. I just want to be sure that this is the right thing for both of us."

Jason's eyes became bright and purposeful. "It is for me. I knew the moment you came running after me with that bus token."

"That was less than three months ago."

"Talkativeness," Jason told her severely, "is a terrible trait in a woman. Nevertheless, I am willing to overlook it."

He held out his arms, and Sandy melted into them with a sense of coming home.

"I know this is right," he said, "for both of us. You'll see."

A